DUDE

by

Nick DiMartino

Photography by David French

University Book Store Press
Seattle, Washington

DUDE
Copyright © 2011 by Nick DiMartino
Photographs of Dude © 2011 by David French
Photographs of Buddy © 2011 by Jacob Monderen
Anna Micklin, publishing coordinator
Brad Herst, technical consultant

UNIVERSITY BOOK STORE PRESS
Espresso Book Machine
First Printing: November 2011

This is entirely a work of fiction.
All rights reserved.

ISBN: 978-1-937358-06-8

UNIVERSITY BOOK STORE
4326 University Way NE
Seattle, Washington 98105
www.ubookstore.com
206-634-3400

For autographed copies, with free shipping, call:
206-543-5896

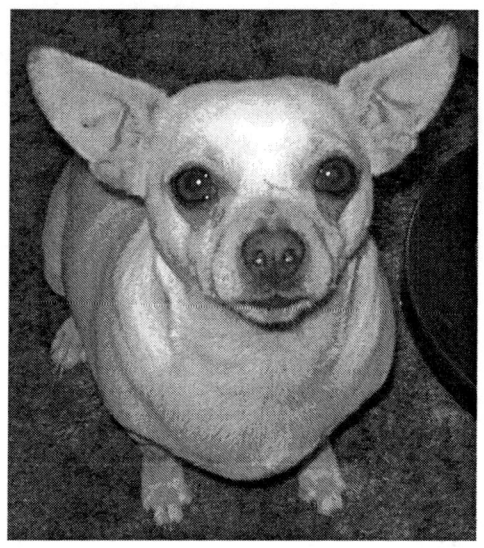

PART ONE

Chapter 1
A Scratching at the Door

My first clue that something alive was trapped on the other side of that door was the sound of scratching.

The second floor hallway should have been hushed and lifeless at that time of the morning, just the creak of the old floorboards under the weight of my feet, the occasional whoosh of the water heater. I stopped in my tracks and listened again.

It wasn't the Stolls. Their radio wasn't on. Whenever they were up and about, you could hear their radio softly tinkling away. The elderly German couple downstairs were my landlords. I didn't think they were home. They were early-risers and often went on vigorous walks in the morning. Besides, the sound wasn't coming from below.

The sound was on this floor.

Which didn't make sense. No one else was home. Rudy had left early for Value Village to steal a few clothes. I knew Taylor wasn't home because I'd heard his car engine early that morning grumbling and snorting outside my bedroom window. They were the only other two renters besides me, so who could be making that noise? There just wasn't anyone else left in the house – human, that is.

My thoughts shifted to other possibilities. I shuddered to think there could be rats in the walls. If I were living in a basement apartment that would be more likely, but the second floor seemed a little high for rodent infestation. Still, it wouldn't be the first time I'd lived in a University District rental and had to battle my rodent brothers to claim the turf. You're only squeamish at first. Then you realize it's a fight for survival. I have beaten a rat to death with a fireplace poker. Admittedly, my eyes were closed. Admittedly, he had a mousetrap clamped to his tail. Admittedly, he was trapped in my cupboard. Nevertheless, when desperate, with my back to the wall, I can fight.

I listened.

There it was again. Scratching, frantic scratching, and soft thuds striking and rattling Taylor's door. Something was whining miserably, desperately clawing at the wood on the other side.

Something wanted out, something too large to be a rat.

"That's got to be a dog," I concluded. "Taylor has some overnight guest in there with a dog," I was growing more and more certain. "Of course, that's what it is. What else could it be? His guest is probably loaded on drugs and they've forgotten to feed the poor pooch."

The soft thrashing sound continued, punctuated with scratch-scratch, scratch-scratch. "Of course, it's a dog," I thought. "At least, I hope it's a dog." The bleak alternatives made me shudder. "Because if it's not a dog…"

I didn't put anything past Taylor Gates.

It didn't take much imagination to visualize someone bound and gagged, kicking and scratching feebly at the door, a human victim incapacitated and waiting to be tortured. That was enough to make me hurry out the door at the end of the hallway and down the outside stairs. If someone was bound and gagged in Taylor's apartment and guarded by a vicious dog, the last thing I wanted was to be caught outside listening. Taylor Gates had some very creepy friends, and I had a bus to catch.

Taylor was someone I avoided. All kinds of shady, morally questionable people visited him, and they talked in the hall outside my door. I'd heard him brag about robbing a grocery store. I'd overheard the lurid details of drug parties. Taylor had done just about everything you can do, except kill a man. That he hadn't done yet. Or so he'd claimed once, with a laugh.

This guy exuded an almost palpable sense of darkness, of no moral boundaries, of – well, I hate to say evil, but the word applies. Every ounce of intuition inside me shouted to stay out of his way, this guy can only bring you trouble. From the day I moved in, the very first moment I saw Taylor Gates step out of his door, shirt off as usual, letting the world get a good look at him, my trustworthy inner alarm went off: danger! danger!

I should admit right now, this guy was very good-looking, which was probably why he was so screwed up. The world never waits long before corrupting physically attractive people, and Taylor Gates had a lot to corrupt.

He couldn't have weighed more than a hundred and sixty pounds, he was tight and supple as a teenager, just a little softer. He liked to lounge around the television room in a wifebeater and pajama bottoms, and though his defiant eroticism had at first been attractive, there was an attitude about Taylor which in time obscured his physical beauty and made you look elsewhere.

His razor of a smile could instantly evaluate you. He had such an immediate sense of all my personal inner failings that I could hardly look him in the eye. He saw through all my defenses. He'd say something like, "It's not what you're thinking," and I'd be unnerved because there was no way he could have known what I was thinking. Most of the time he pretended to be laid back and good-natured, but it wasn't long before I got to see firsthand how quickly he could lose his temper and become terrifying.

Whenever our paths crossed in the hall or on the stairs he was usually answering a call on his cell or making one. From the sheer number of calls he constantly got and his short, curt answers, it didn't take a detective to figure out that he was probably a drug dealer of some kind, maybe marijuana, maybe it was nothing worse than that. Unfortunately, my gut instincts told me he wasn't quite laid back enough to be selling bud. More likely cocaine.

Hopefully not crystal meth or heroin.

He seemed proud that he'd been involved in a number of petty crimes, because whenever I heard him talking to his friends in the hallway, sooner or later he would proudly mention his "licks," as he called them. He gleefully narrated tales of near escapes from the law and brief, ugly violence. Once he casually mentioned that in jail all you watched was the African-American channel on television, because the black prisoners dominated the selection. It sounded like he was talking from experience. Yet he was clearly able to look the part of the well-behaved good boy convincingly enough that he had fooled canny Mrs Stoll into signing his lease.

I hurried down the stairs and jogged over to the bus stop, catching the bus just as it was pulling away, so I wasn't late to work. But no matter how I tried to relax, I couldn't shake the uncomfortable feeling that something alive was imprisoned in Taylor's room.

That night, coming home from the bookstore, as I got to the top of the stairs and started past his door, I heard the same scratching and whimpering. I hesitated, listening intently for any other sound. Then I took a step closer. Something sensed my presence and thudded loudly against the door, whining and clawing.

I stepped back with a flinch, then hurried down the hall to my own door, and locked it behind me.

"Okay, it's not a human being, that's for sure," I thought. "That was an animal, no doubt about it. Probably a dog. But why would a dog be locked in Taylor's apartment all day? Just what is that guy guarding in there?" I couldn't help but wonder if the dog was vicious.

It could belong to anyone. All day long dangerous-looking young people went in and out of his room, as often as not wearing clothes that hadn't seen a laundromat for weeks. Taylor never lacked for quickly-made friends of both sexes, all eager to get him alone and high – and undressed, I suspected – but none of them ever came back more than once or twice. Taylor wore people out. I'd heard the muffled angry voices of more than one fight with disappointed, frustrated would-be partners, from all the way down at the other end of the hall.

Now there was a new sound.

An animal's feeble, frustrated escape attempts.

I drew aside the window curtains enough to see that Taylor's car was still missing from its usual spot behind the apartment house. He'd been gone all day, doing whatever he did with his time.

I opened my apartment door, took a couple quiet steps into the hallway, and listened. More scratching, followed by a scared, protesting yelp. That's all it took to get me halfway down the hall, ready to meddle in affairs that were none of my business.

The door between Taylor's room and mine jerked open. I froze in my tracks. It was my pale, skinny neighbor, Rudy, hastily wrapped in his shabby white bathrobe, red-eyed and stubbly-chinned, his hair rooster-tailing and pillow-matted, looking like he'd just crawled out of bed in the middle of the afternoon. Which he probably had.

"Oh, it's you," he said, making no attempt to hide his disappointment. "I thought Taylor was home."

He looked genuinely disappointed in me for not being Taylor. With a clenched jaw and tightly pursed lips, he lingered there anxiously, his own door open, staring at Taylor's apartment.

"He should have been home by now."

I had nothing to say to that.

I retreated awkwardly, confused and embarrassed, into my own apartment and closed the door behind me, leaving Rudy out in the hallway, waiting and hoping. Dismissing the whole thing from my mind as none of my business, I took off my jacket, unpacked my backpack, tugged off my shoes and sat down in front of my computer. There I focused on writing an extraordinary book review about a rather ordinary book, and let the drone of my electric heater drown out any further noises from down the hall.

Chapter 2
When the Door Opens

I've never had a dog, and I've had three cats. My life has been measured in cats. My last cat was the best of them all. For twelve years Buddy was the most faithful companion I'd ever had, handsome and affectionate and fun.

Then he stopped eating. The woman veterinarian paying house calls diagnosed my poor ailing Buddy with intestinal cancer. I was forced to watch helplessly as he grew weaker and weaker. Five weeks later he died. I lay beside him on the bed during his last eight hours, and buried him in his favorite part of the back yard.

Losing my beloved Buddy was traumatic in every sense of the word. His passing left me morbidly depressed. We had developed something very pure between us, a mutual respect and love that were profound. I was lost without him. I couldn't emotionally get back on my feet.

I forgot how to laugh. I dreaded coming home from work. I didn't answer the phone. I didn't answer my emails. I was embarrassed to let anyone see how upset I was over losing what others might call a mere cat. I sank into a hopeless darkness and stopped believing I could ever climb out. The crying jags were mortifying. The slightest thing could make me lose control.

My parents were worried sick and baffled. "All this over a cat?" said my mother. "Just get another one."

They were not alone. Well-meaning family and friends filled my mailbox with sympathy cards full of the usual advice. There was only one solution to losing a pet. Immediately replace it with another pet, adopt another cat at once, quickly fill the gap in my life with the love and distractions of a new feline friend. As though one cat could simply be substituted for another! It was impossible for me to even think of replacing Buddy. No other cat would ever comfort me.

Finally one Sunday morning someone started banging on my door and wouldn't stop. It was my friend, Jacob, who pushed past me into the apartment, pulled back the curtains to let in some light, opened a window to let in some air, and sat me down to talk some sense into me.

"Look at this place," he said. "You live in a mausoleum. Pictures of Buddy everywhere. You haven't put away his food bowl. You've still got that damn scratching post, and his bedmat on the armchair. You're not moving on here. You're not writing anymore. You don't go to movies. You don't see your friends. You've given up on life. Come on, snap out of it."

"I can't. Everywhere I look, I still see him…"

"Then you need to get out of here."

"But where would I go?"

"Where? There's a perfect place just waiting for you to move in. All we have to do is find it. Come on, you and I are going to do some serious apartment hunting."

He was right. I really had no choice but to start over, to pack up and get out of that apartment. I had to leave the memories behind me. Whenever you lose someone dear, you're always left wrestling with the realization that you are doomed to lose everyone else as well. Losing Buddy was only a taste of what was in store for me. Life would be a long parade of funerals.

Moving away from that apartment I had shared with Buddy was the single act that saved my sanity. A wonderful, tiny new apartment turned out to be the perfect place to begin over again, upstairs in a spacious two-story carpenter cottage in a lovely old neighborhood in the University District, on a quiet avenue lined with maple trees.

When I woke up the next day, I made the same mistake I made every morning. I lay in bed without moving my legs, being careful not to accidentally kick Buddy curled up at the foot of the bed. I had to remind myself, once again, that I could move my legs now, that there was no longer any danger of disturbing him.

I made myself think of other things, caught the early bus to campus, and put in a half shift at the bookstore. At home I finished writing a book review, then took a bleak look into my refrigerator, which was enough to convince me that I'd have to take a walk to the supermarket before I could cook any kind of dinner.

I'll admit, I was curious whether I'd hear anything in Taylor's room as I locked my door behind me. I hardly had time to take one step down the hall before his door flew open and he came charging out in a headlong dash. He grunted out a curt greeting in my direction, then flung open the hallway door and clattered down the stairs toward a car that was idling behind our apartment house.

I watched from the top of the stairs as the car pulled out of its parking place. Then I stepped back into the hall. Taylor had left his door wide open. He was gone. The car had driven away. All I had to do was take three steps, and I would be standing right in front of the open doorway, looking into his apartment.

I took three steps.

He hadn't turned off his television set. An action-movie car chase dominated the big screen, on mute, wheels screeching by in silence. An open pizza box gaped on the coffee table, with one slice left. Clothing was flung everywhere, legs and sleeves scattered where they had fallen. Sections of newspaper, unwashed dishes, loose change, candy wrappers, and a shoulder-bag littered the floor.

I took half a dozen hesitant steps into the disorder. Through one door I saw into his bathroom. A towel was draped over the shower curtain bar. A shaver was balanced on the edge of the sink, next to an empty tube of toothpaste. Pill bottles lined the glass shelf beneath the dirty mirror.

Through the open bedroom doorway I looked in on rumpled blankets and a bedspread half-fallen off an unmade bed. With wildly pounding heart, listening for the sound of anyone approaching, I was retreating back toward the hallway, careful not to trip over his slippers, when I thought I saw something move on the bed.

I looked again.

A blanket shifted.

From underneath the heap of quilts and fleeces protruded the black tip of a small nose.

A car door slammed down below in the parking lot.

I heard Taylor's voice call, "Have a good one, bro," as the battered excuse of a car grumbled away.

I bolted out of Taylor's apartment and in my panic, instead of leaving the door open as I'd found it, I let the door slam shut behind me. With a groan at my own stupidity, I dashed down the hall into my apartment and locked the door behind me, all thought of walking to the supermarket abandoned.

I heard Taylor's door open and close.

That night I went to bed without dinner.

Chapter 3

A Taste of His Rage

Not long after that I got my first taste of Taylor's rage.

It was a sweltering hot evening. The door at the end of the hallway was propped open trying to suck inside any passing breeze. I had given up on wearing anything more than my jockey shorts and undershirt, and was sitting at my computer pounding on the keyboard, trying to write a book review and hoping I had something to say.

Although I could hear Taylor down the hall yelling at someone, I was doing my best to ignore him and focus on my writing. That his angry swearing was slowly getting louder didn't dawn on me until later. That he could possibly be yelling at me did not even occur to me.

I finally decided I'd had enough and was getting to my feet to close the door, determined to sacrifice any hope of cool air in exchange for blocking out that unpleasant spewing of verbal ugliness, when I suddenly found myself face to face with him, and realized he was actually inside my home.

I was so floored by his invasion that I was speechless. He wasn't waiting for me to say anything, anyway. "What the fuck were you doing in my apartment?" he shouted.

I was so dumbfounded by the accusation that my voice squeaked. "I wasn't in your apartment." I rose to my feet in indignation, forgetting as I defiantly faced the intruder that I was only wearing my underwear.

"Oh, no?" he said. "You didn't just step in there while I was gone?" His laugh was aggressive and threatening. "Gee, then I wonder who stole my drugs?"

Afterward it's always easy to think of clever repartee. At the time, I was left sputtering, so thunderstruck that nothing witty occurred to me.

"What are you talking about?" was the best I could manage to say. "Why would I steal your drugs?"

"Why? Why?" That sparked another spewing of cold-blooded laughter. "I'll tell you why. An eight-ball of black tar heroin, that's why. It was sitting very nicely on my desk and now it seems to have walked off."

"What does that have to do with me?"

His face was bloodshot with anger. "Give it back before I rip this place apart looking for it."

"Whatever you're looking for, it's not here," I blurted out. The words were no sooner out of my mouth than I regretted them. I was only making it worse.

He seemed to take one big step in my direction, and suddenly he was bumping into me, chest to chest, my back pressed up against the wall, the front of my undershirt bunched in his fist.

"You're the only one who could have taken it, you motherfucker. Now, where is it?"

He nearly jerked me off my feet and was about to slam the back of my head against the wall when the angry barking of some ferocious beast erupted at ear-splitting volume behind him. We were obviously in danger of being ripped to pieces by something savage lunging toward us from the hall. I strained to see past him over his shoulder. He spun around to see where I was looking.

A huge guinea pig the size of a cat with ears as big as its head and the bulging black eyes of a giant frog was standing in the doorway. That was the best my overwrought imagination could do with the facts. I blinked. It wasn't an hallucination. There was no sign of the killer mastiff threatening to devour us.

The hound of the Baskervilles with his house-shaking barks was nothing more than a tiny gold-and-white Chihuahua. There he stood, looking as fierce as he could, on his bony little bird legs, with the oversize ears of a bat and the coiling tail of a pig.

A long strip of cellophane was caught on one of the little dog's teeth, and hung down the side of his mouth like a dead snake. Dangling from the end of the thin strip of plastic was stuck a black glob that looked like a wad of very old chewing gum.

I had a feeling it wasn't chewing gum.

Chapter 4
Apologies and Introductions

"Sorry about what happened yesterday."

Taylor was standing shirtless outside my door with the little Chihuahua in his arms, nestled up against his bare skin. Ears flattened down warily, the little head on that great big neck was swiveling around in all directions, trying to guess where danger would be coming from next.

"It can happen," I said lamely. What could I say? After yesterday, I no longer trusted him. As far as I was concerned, I had seen my sinister housemate completely lose touch with reality and become violent, all on a misunderstanding, all over a substance that had led more than one person down a dark and ugly road. "You've got me totally wrong if you think I would ever steal anyone's drugs."

"I'll never think it again." He patted my arm reassuringly. "I just never dreamed this little thief here could pull off something like that."

"Well, you had no business thinking it was me." I was still far from mollified. I'd never seen heroin before, but by the way Taylor had snatched the black wad away from that little pooch, the mystery of who stole it had been solved.

"You haven't met my new dog yet," said Taylor, artfully changing the subject, stepping closer so that his bare arm brushed up against me and turning slightly so that the Chihuahua's face and my face were inches apart. Before I knew enough to back away, the little dog's tongue shot out of his mouth and lapped me across the lips.

"Hey, Dude, stop kissing my neighbor," said Taylor, at his most charming. "You've gotta watch this guy. He's got a real thing about kissing."

He moved Dude a little closer to me, and this time I was smart enough to back away out of tongue range.

"I had no business accusing you. That was shitty."

His apology rang hollow. I got the feeling he wasn't very good at apologizing, probably due to not doing it very often. I wondered briefly why he was standing half-naked in my doorway saying he was sorry. A moment later his motive became clear. "Say, I wonder if you could do me a favor."

I tried not to let the cute dog distract me.

"Mrs Stoll says that Dude was barking all day yesterday while I was gone," said Taylor. "I guess she got a phone call from that old bitch who lives in the house next door."

"I didn't hear any barking," I said, attempting to absolve myself of guilt in advance. "He never bothers me."

"Well, that's great," he said, trying not to let my interruption break the momentum of his request. "He just gets scared, that's all, being in this big new place all alone. So the problem is, I gotta leave for about two hours now, I just gotta go, there's no way out of it, and I can't bring him with me. So I was wondering…"

He held out Dude toward me.

I put up my hands to ward him off. "Not me, no, no, no. You've got the wrong guy. I don't know a thing about dogs." I tried to laugh disparagingly. "I'm a cat person. I grew up with cats. I understand cats. Dogs are unknown territory. I'm no dog sitter. Why don't you ask Rudy?"

"Rudy is too stoned to know his head from his ass," he said bluntly, quickly softening his words with a confidential smile, implying that I was a different kind of person altogether, that he would never say such a thing about me. "I don't trust Rudy with my most precious possession."

He paused. I got the feeling he was weighing just how far he could trust me. "See, the thing is, dogs aren't allowed here. Old lady Stoll would not be happy if she found out Dude was mine. She lets Rudy keep that horrible bitch of a cat, leaving her stinky piss all over, always meowing at the door.

But no dogs. So I told her Dude belongs to a friend, and only visits once in a while. I gotta make sure he keeps his yap shut from now on, see, and the problem is, he freaks out when he's alone. Here, take him. Go ahead, hold him."

This time when he thrust the dog toward me, I took Dude into my arms. He immediately stuck his tongue between my lips and then up my nostril.

"He likes you."

"Really, how can you tell?"

"He likes your taste, don't you, Dude? Dogs can tell a lot about you by your taste. And when a dog licks your lips, dogs have such super-sensitive taste buds, he can tell the last thing that you ate."

An uncomfortable thought! I tried to remember the last thing I'd eaten, and wondered if Dude had tasted it.

"Treat him nice, Dude," he said, scratching the dog behind the ears. "Not too much licking, now. You don't want to scare him off before you even get to know each other." He backed away, leaving Dude in my arms, edging toward the doorway. "I really appreciate this, bro. I'll only be gone a couple hours, tops. All you have to do is let him hang out in your apartment. He just needs company, so he won't get scared. He's taken a pee. He's had his lunch. You'll see, dogs are easy. They practically take care of themselves."

Chapter 5
Babysitting a Dog

Taylor Gates did not come back in two hours.

He came back late that night, sometime after one. By that time I'd endured a hearty dose of dog ownership, and that sampling was more than enough. I'd done a favor for a housemate, but I was thoroughly relieved to return that little four-footed terror to his rightful owner. I had never been alone that long with a dog before. I had figured it would be a lot like being alone with a cat.

Chihuahuas are not like cats.

That afternoon alone with Dude was an ordeal in awkward frustration. What did he want from me, this goofy little joke of an animal? Why wouldn't he leave me alone? What did he expect from me?

I decided to act as normal as possible, and let the Chihuahua adapt to me. I settled into my armchair, opened the novel I was currently reviewing, and started reading. After a couple pages, I looked up. He was staring at me.

I read another page, and glanced up again.

Still staring.

He kept watching me like I was a time bomb ready to go off, his curly little tail wagging eagerly. If I got up from my chair for any reason, to get a drink or go to the bathroom, he'd either follow on my heels or I'd come back to find him sitting in my place. If I spoke a word to him, any word, he took that as a go-ahead to rear up on his hind legs, put his two front paws on my knee, and strain to get within licking distance. When I tried to move away, he anticipated me and dashed to get there first.

I focused my eyes on the book and forced them to move slowly down the page. I did not look up, I did not look up. I looked up. Still staring.

I closed my book in frustration. Okay, that wasn't going to work.

I got out of my armchair, stepped over him and around him, and settled in behind my computer monitor, where I began adding the finishing touches to an overdue book review. The moment I turned away from the screen to check the spelling of a character's name in the book, he jumped uninvited into my lap, where he lavished affection on me, trying to convince me to let him stay, making me reach around him to strike the right keys on the keyboard, trying to rest his chin on my forearm while I typed.

Before long he was squirming, shifting position, and staring up at me with his bulging, mournful eyes. He seemed to be pleading for understanding, insisting that it wasn't his fault if he was born with enough energy to power five dogs twice his size. He had no idea how to downshift into a slower gear. He radiated boundless enthusiasm, bug-eyed with joy, a thundering express train with nowhere to go. All he could do was shiver with excitement, and then try to slowly claw his way up my chest, possessed with eagerness to get within licking distance of my cheek.

"Whoa, hold on there, pardner...!"

In a moment he was all over me, this solid little meatloaf of a pooch, his custard blond, perfectly-shaped head just slightly too small for his thick, meaty neck. His legs were thin and delicate, skin-covered bird-bones ending in what looked more like a chicken claw than a paw. His huge ears and curly little tail added a court jester touch.

He leaped from my lap, did a mad, galloping dash around my writing desk, and came to a sudden halt by my side, looking up expectantly, like a basketball player ready to pass the ball in any direction, wagging his tail intensely.

Boing, and he was in my lap again, squirming to secure his position, pretending to chew on my fingers. He bumped me with his head, and I accidentally hit a wrong letter. Unrepentant, he bumped my hand again. Damn, another wrong letter. Dude, stop bumping me. But he only had one overriding goal, to persuade me to stop typing and focus my attention on him, where it belonged.

I clicked on Save and stood up. Enough!

Every time I turned around, there he was.

"What are you staring at?" I cried at last, in exasperation. Those big, black eyes of his, bugging out of his head like an insect's, had been focused on one thing, and one thing alone, all afternoon and evening and into the night: me. He watched me make a sandwich. He watched me take my pills. He watched me shave. He watched me sit on the toilet. I was never offstage with this little character. Suddenly I had an audience of one who was paying continuous rapt attention to every single move I made.

After about three hours he seemed to become distracted, and began doing an odd, shuffling dance by the door and whimpering. Watching him made me nervous. This wasn't supposed to happen. I could think of only one logical interpretation, and very few options.

Finally I opened my apartment door. At once he galloped down the hall to the door at the other end and scratched at the wood, like he was knocking. I strode down the hall after him, and opened that door, too.

Before I could think twice about letting someone else's dog out of the house, Dude bolted out and down the outside back stairs toward the alley.

"Dude, come back here!" I cried in my less than authoritative voice. My limp command got no response. I hurried down the wooden staircase after him. By the time I reached the bottom of the stairs, however, Dude had just finished unleashing a hot little stream on the corner of the house. Leaving a yellow puddle behind him, he was on his way back up.

"Good boy," I cooed, thoroughly impressed.

Dinner was another issue. How long was he supposed to go without eating? How could I cook anything with him watching me, and not share?

I shared.

As the clock neared ten, in exasperation I gave up on my third attempt to read a book. He was sitting on the floor at my feet, and the moment I closed it he leaped into my lap where he turned around in a circle and then lay down with an exhausted sigh. I was stunned. I didn't move. Without meaning to, I let my eyes close…

I was startled awake by the door at the end of the hall banging open. Dude leaped off my lap, raced to the door and began pawing at it, trying to get out.

I swung it open before Taylor had time to knock.

"Hey, I'm a little late. Hope that's not a problem."

I glanced at my watch. 1:15 a.m.

"Damn Mexicans don't understand being on time. Hey there, how's it goin', little guy?"

I could tell he was ripped on something. His eyes were glazed and his lower jaw kept shifting back and forth. He was wired, his foot was tapping, he couldn't stand still. His shirt was untucked and there were big sweat stains under his armpits.

"How's my boy?" he said, scooping up Dude in his arms and letting the dog lick him all over his face. "You been a good boy, Dude? Did you show your good manners? Did you make a new friend?"

Chapter 6

Servant to the Princess

A few days later, on a gray, overcast morning, as I was taking the garbage down the back stairs, Mrs Stoll opened her kitchen door and poked her head out. "Do you have a moment?" she said. "Do you know if Mr Rudy is sick."

"Sick?" I couldn't remember seeing him recently. I tried to think back if I had heard any coughing or sneezing next door. "Not that I know of. Why?"

"I have not seen him for two days. We do not hear his footsteps on our ceiling. Can you look for me?"

I assured Mrs Stoll I'd find out for her, and after throwing my bag of trash into the big green bin in the alley, I headed up the stairs to take care of it at once. I was so focused on Rudy's door and what I was going to say to explain my knocking that I tripped and nearly fell over his cat.

She's a big gray beauty, spoiled and grumpy on the best of days. She yowled at me royally, hissed, and backed away, just as Rudy opened his door and said, "Princess?" That was all it took for her to scamper dramatically inside, as though escaping from being molested.

"Was she trying to get out?" he asked.

"I'm not sure," I floundered. "I didn't see her. That was the problem."

"She's so unhappy," he said, with what sounded like real regret.

"Are you okay, Rudy?" I asked.

Rudy Flowers had never looked like a paragon of health as long as I'd lived there, but he was definitely looking worse, with cavernous eye sockets and gaunt, blood-drained cheeks. His skinny body was wrapped in that dingy white bathrobe. It fell open on a dingy white T-shirt. His hair, as usual, was still flattened from his pillow in various directions, like the broken antennae of an alien.

He really wouldn't have been bad looking if he'd only taken care of himself. He was somewhere in his thirties, although sometimes he looked like a weathered, homeless man in his late forties. At other times his face had a confused boyish innocence, a kind of Huck Finn charm, so that he looked about fourteen. Lanky and flexible, he had a funny bowlegged walk that was almost a strut. His flat, bare feet hugged the wooden floor like a duck's.

He didn't seem to hear my question, or else didn't believe it warranted an answer. His thoughts were focused on Princess, and that's where they remained.

"She keeps trying to get out," he whined. "I used to let her outside, when the weather was nice. But now the first thing she does is eat grass, and then she throws up. So I can't let her go outside anymore. And that makes her so unhappy! All day long she tries to find ways to escape."

We ran out of things to say, so I decided to cut it short. "Well, sorry to bother you."

"You weren't bothering me."

"Mrs Stoll was afraid you were sick."

Again he didn't seem to hear me. "I'm so rude," he said, stepping back. "I've never invited you inside. Some neighbor I am! Please, let me prove to you that I'm not a complete jerk."

I didn't see a way out of it, and so I hesitantly followed him into his apartment. He locked the door behind us.

Then he led me down a bookshelf-lined hall that smelled of dust and cat pee into a small living room crowded with secondhand furniture and lined with walls full of books. It was mostly one big library and movie room with a bed sandwiched in as an afterthought, a claustrophobic hoarding of a zillion paperbacks, occasionally interrupted by towering piles of DVDs, and three struggling little windows half-blocked by half a dozen slip-sleeved comic book collections. A big, comfortable-looking well-padded armchair nestled in the middle of this little pleasure cave, where he clearly spent most of his waking hours, watching his favorite police procedurals and true crime dramas on television, or reading science-fiction thrillers, or thumbing through issue after issue of superhero comics, or playing violent killing games on his PlayStation 2.

Though the sun was shining outside, the shades were all drawn so that the room was in a dim artificial twilight. On top of a small table, on a stack of books, an incense stick was just flickering out.

"Princess?"

No sign of her. He seemed to know all her hiding places, and discreetly glanced in each of them.

Princess was nowhere to be found.

"I bought her this new little fountain," he said, pointing down to a burbling, blue water dish in the corner with a tiny spout constantly splashing up in the middle. "Some cats only drink water that's moving, you know."

"Buddy was like that," I said, eager to show my understanding of cats. "He would only drink from dripping faucets."

"I didn't know you had a cat, too."

"Not any more," I had to admit. "Buddy passed away. I live by myself now."

Clearly the topic made him uncomfortable. He changed it, continuing to look down at the cat's new water bowl with regret. "I worry about Princess. She doesn't drink enough water. I don't want her to get dehydrated. I thought she would like her little fountain."

As though on cue, Princess appeared out of nowhere and walked past her new water bowl as though it were beneath contempt, disdaining to even glance at such an insipid idea.

"She hasn't been eating right lately," said Rudy. "I think it's a digestion issue. I think that's why she eats grass. There's a free clinic at the Humane Society in a month. I'm going to take her. She'll hate it."

He opened his refrigerator door and took out a carefully-covered can half-filled with cat food, which he chopped into bite-size chunks with a spoon. He then scooped it down into the bowl next to her water fountain. "Here, Princess!" he called in an unexpected falsetto. "Here, girl!"

He looked expectantly toward the room where she'd vanished. "Dinner time, Princess. Your favorite tonight, honey. Yummy white fish, just the way you like it. Come on, sweetie, time to eat."

No response.

"Here, girlie-girl!" he began again, calling her in a high-pitched child's voice. "Pretty, pretty girl."

I backed toward the door to the hall. Rudy scarcely seemed to notice I was leaving. He was too busy trying to convince Princess to enjoy her cat food.

Chapter 7
Jade

I could see that Rudy Flowers was lonely. Anyone could see that. He didn't have any friends visiting, or parents dropping by. His only relationship appeared to be with his cat, supplemented by the occasional visit from Taylor or myself. I soon figured out from the mail arriving that he was living on Unemployment checks and food stamps. As far as I could see, he seemed to wait every Tuesday for the mailman to bring his check, he would dash to the bank, spend a lot of time with Taylor for a couple days, and then go back into seclusion.

Most days of the week Rudy didn't leave his room much. In the evening, as often as not, I'd find him waiting for me to come home from the bookstore, another human being to populate his solitary world. I'd trudge wearily up the back stairs and into the hallway to find his door open invitingly. He always made me green tea, prepared just the way I like it, with lots of sugar. He would offer me his bong, stuffed with the highest grade medical marijuana. He would put a plate of crackers on the coffee table, the kind of crackers they give away at the food bank.

Then one afternoon I came home from work to find Princess outside, enjoying herself on the porch where she was forbidden to go, and her master inside, completely unaware of her transgression, his bathrobe flaring behind him as he stormed back and forth, pacing the hall in a fury, mumbling to himself, trying to exorcise his anger.

"Rudy, what's wrong?" How could I say anything else? He was a perfect study in misery.

"What's wrong?" he repeated, stopping long enough to face me. "I'll tell you what's wrong. I didn't get my wake-up, that's what's wrong. That jerk is going back on his word, that's what's wrong. One of his customers, you haven't met her, is this seventeen-year-old brat..."

"Wait, wait, wait. Who are you talking about?"

"Taylor, obviously."

"What do you mean, customers?" In his pent-up frustration, Rudy was assuming I knew more than I did.

"You must have figured it out by now. Taylor is a dealer."

"I'll admit, I considered the possibility..."

"Yeah, and well, you've probably figured out by now that I've got a little bit of a habit – well, okay, it's not so little. I have a need, a serious, daily need – and he promised me that for half of my weekly check he'd keep me high all week. I wouldn't have to worry about morning wake-ups anymore. And it was sweet for a while, for the first couple weeks, I'd just trot over next door every morning and get what I needed, and the day would take care of itself. Which was fine until one of his regular customers, this high school chick with a habit..."

High school? Heroin? I groaned. Another brave new generation of high schoolers discovering the old grand-daddy of nasty habits. I was so grateful for my own narrow escape from drug addiction that hearing about her drug choice so early in life made me ache for her. I missed some of what Rudy was saying, and re-connected with him mid-sentence.

"...and so she's starting to call Taylor every day to get more stuff, but then she's running out of money and her father has caught her taking bills out of his wallet and so Taylor starts giving her free stuff so she'll put out. Two days after her eighteenth birthday she lets him go all the way. They were at it all night. I could hear them through the wall."

He paused for a moment, as though he could still hear them. The memory clearly repulsed him.

"So it isn't long before she starts spending the night, shooting up what I'm expecting to do the next morning. My stuff! Mine! *Mine!* Today I didn't get my wake-up in the morning again, and why? Because she was here last night. Now he's always running short. And he keeps giving me one bullshit excuse after another. Why bother? It's no mystery. The one who gets it is her. And you know who goes without? You know who the loser is in this little arrangement? Me."

"Then stop giving him your money!" I said indignantly.

He sadly shook his head. "Yeah, I could do that, I suppose. But then for sure I'll have to go without. With Taylor I can at least hope. I've got to give him my money. He's the only chance I've got."

Not long after that I caught my first sight of her. I was walking down the outside staircase toward a late morning shift at the bookstore. She and Taylor were just coming up the stairs toward me, red-eyed and exhausted, bringing to a close a wild night they'd enjoyed somewhere else, slowly shuffling up toward Taylor's place to crash.

Halfway down the stairs, we passed each other. She looked vaguely familiar, prettier than most, younger than most. She was a slim, delicate thing with big, brown eyes and shoulder-length hair. Taylor grunted a greeting in my direction but didn't introduce her. She gave me a quick, shy smile in passing. It went right to my heart, and I found myself aching for her and fearing.

Chapter 8
At the Rescue Shelter

As the days got warmer, Taylor's business picked up. His cell phone was ringing constantly. He made more deliveries and spent more time with Jade. Dude was left in the care of Rudy and I.

Which was just great with us.

Instead of trudging up the back stairs exhausted after a day working at the bookstore, I would bound up the back stairs eagerly hoping that Rudy's or Taylor's door would be open, and that I would get another chance to enjoy one of Dude's ecstatic, tail-wagging welcomes.

"How's my big boy?" I'd cry. "How's it goin', Dude?"

He would rear up on his hind legs, put his front paws on my knee, and strain upward to lick my hand and be patted on the head, his little tail wagging in a frenzy.

No matter how exhausted and psychologically bruised I might be from my day at the bookstore, all I needed was to see Dude charging toward me to forget all about it. Sometimes I'd share an afternoon cup of yogurt with him. Sometimes we'd go over and visit Rudy next door, and over green tea and crackers and medical marijuana, we'd both listen to Rudy chatter away.

Since Rudy didn't work, on the days when I had shifts at the bookstore he would take charge of Dude, letting him out to do his business, or brushing him, or playing with him, or napping with him. Dude enjoyed visiting Rudy's apartment and made himself completely at home there, ignoring the hatred glaring at him from the green eyes of the offended Princess.

Once Rudy was loaded, I could usually get him talking about anything. "What I don't understand is why Taylor ever wanted a dog, in the first place?"

"Of course you don't understand it," he said, blowing out bong smoke, "because it doesn't make any sense."

"Seems to me just feeding a dog would be a daily hassle," I pointed out, "not to mention an expense he couldn't afford, not to mention a restriction on his mobility."

"Of course it was," he agreed with me, "all of those losses and more, one big minus after another! Plus the cost of buying the damned thing in the first place. And it couldn't be just a cheap, ordinary mutt – it had to be a Chihuahua. What a ridiculous waste of money! I was against it from the very beginning."

I'd heard Rudy tell the story several times, but he didn't always remember the details. Sometimes he did, but often he left them out, and just held onto the general shape of things. Sometimes if I asked the right questions, I could pry the details out of him.

For instance, I knew they found Dude at a rescue shelter for animals somewhere in Puyallup, but I could never tell which one. I could only do my best to remember what Rudy said, to piece together the best of the various versions and guess at the rest.

Somewhere online one night Taylor and Jade saw a photo of Charlie the Chihuahua, up for adoption. This was back when she was more-of-a-customer and less-of-a-girlfriend. Her excitement over getting a dog was one of the strong arguments in its favor. Charlie looked exactly right for them, compact and warm-hearted and goofy. Jade set her heart on him.

She phoned her father and told him she was staying over at a girlfriend's. That was the first time she ever spent the night. The next morning she and Taylor dragged Rudy out of bed with promises of a wake-up, and the three of them made the long drive to Puyallup.

They were shown to the Chihuahua cage, where they got a good look at the twelve little dogs uncomfortably crowded together, and were introduced to Charlie.

He was ugly, unsociable and unhappy.

Of the dozen Chihuahuas at the rescue center, only one was rambunctiously friendly. Only one acted eager to go home with them. Only one jumped immediately into Taylor's lap, put his front paws on his chest, and licked his face.

"That's the one I want," he said.

Jade was thrilled. She hugged Taylor with excitement, no longer the world-weary twentysomething she pretended to be, but the excited seventeen-year-old she really was. "He's the cutest thing in the world," she exclaimed in delight, crouching down beside Taylor and letting the little dog lick her cheek. "Can we really take this one home with us?" It was exactly the response Taylor had been hoping for.

"He's gonna be our little fella."

"You're not kidding, are you?"

"Would I kid you about something like that?"

"Yes!" She slapped the back of his head, and they both laughed.

"Let's go sign the papers right now," he said, and then paused. "Actually, Rudy, I think you'll have to sign. They're going to ask for ID, and you know I don't have any. Here's the money." He gave Rudy back the two hundred dollars that Rudy had given him for the week's high.

"But if you spend the two hundred here, how will I get my wake-ups?" complained Rudy.

Taylor sighed and smiled, as though dealing with a learning-disabled child. "I told you not to worry," he said. "You just write your name down on that dotted line. I'll take care of the rest." Although Rudy Flowers was the name that went down on the ownership papers, the dog would belong to Taylor Gates.

"I have to ask if there are any children in your household," said the woman at the rescue center. "Chihuahuas are not good with children."

"No children," said Jade.

"Just her," said Taylor.

Jade punched him.

Rudy signed the adoption form and gave the woman the money.

"What's his name?" Jade asked her, while Rudy was fastening a leash around the little dog's neck.

"Well, his official name on paper is August," she said. "But that's a pretty stuffy name for a very friendly, down-to earth dog. Around here everyone calls him Dude."

Chapter 9

A Brief Happiness before the Dark

Jade and Dude immediately became friends.

He trusted her completely, and always heralded her arrival with yelps of pure joy. I began to suspect she came over more to see Dude than to spend time with Taylor. While she was at the house, she and the dog were inseparable. We'd hear Dude barking outside the closed bedroom door when Taylor wanted Jade to himself. Often, when Taylor drove off to take care of his circle of addicts, Jade would stay with Rudy and me, so that we could all play with the dog.

One sunny afternoon while Taylor was out making deliveries and Rudy kept nodding off into little involuntary naps, Jade convinced me to walk with her down to Cowen Park, taking Dude along on a leash. At the park we unfastened the leash and sat on a picnic table together watching him race exuberantly across the rolling lawns, a graceful little torpedo of a dog. We would call him and laugh in delight as he came charging toward us, galloping as fast as his little legs would carry him.

"I don't know what you see in Taylor," I confided in an unexpected moment of trust.

She smiled. "Eye candy. Free drugs."

"I know you're much more mature than your years," I said to her, "but I'm sometimes afraid for you."

"Don't worry, I can take care of myself," she replied, a little too quickly, a little too confidently.

You always like to think that things can work out. For a couple happy weeks, Taylor and Jade, Rudy and Dude became an ensemble and sometimes they let me join them, riding around together, getting high together, pulling into fast food franchises and eating like irresponsible teenagers, waiting together for the Mexican. The ugliness of what people can do for drugs was momentarily forgotten, the lying and cheating and backstabbing subsumed in the joy of friendship.

That happy moment didn't last.

Money became a problem. Finances never completely recovered from the big Chihuahua purchase. Taylor kept running out of enough money to buy product from the

Mexican. Without something to sell, there was only one other method short of getting a job to provide funds.

The conversations in the car began to change. Dude and I would sit together in a corner of the back seat and listen. I began to see how inseparably drugs and crime were locked in their own nasty little dance of necessity. There was no way out. You needed the drug. You did what you had to do.

Desperate schemes for money-making became the constant topic of conversation – in other words, who to rob and when to do it – some of which were just hot air and raw drug need talking, most of which were smartly discarded before they failed.

But not all.

Chapter 10
The Licks

For a couple days I noticed I was being left out of the conversation. I'd be playing with Dude on the floor and then notice that Rudy and Taylor and Jade were talking together too softly to be heard. Or we'd be getting gas for Taylor's gas-guzzler somewhere, and I'd walk in and join the three of them in the Mini-mart, and they would abruptly stop talking with funny looks on their faces.

Finally one afternoon Rudy smoked a little more than usual, and it loosened up his tongue. We were playing with the dog, and Dude was happily bounding from lap to lap. I asked him why they didn't trust me anymore, and caught him off-guard. He broke down and admitted that trust had become a problem, and after a few false starts finally confessed that Taylor had talked him into being "his getaway driver."

"Being his what?" Just hearing him say the words made me a little sick to my stomach. I was afraid to find out more, but too curious to resist. When he didn't look like he was going to continue the story, I gave him a nudge.

"Getaway from what?" I persisted.

Slowly it all came out, with a bong now and then to help him over the difficult spots. I was horrified to realize I'd been completely oblivious to the transformation that had come over our little group of friends. Taylor had lived up to his word. He had actually proved himself as bad as he'd bragged. He had held up a small grocery store. He had taken everything the little Asian woman had in the till, which amounted to less than two hundred dollars.

"He held her up at gunpoint," said Rudy, "but the thing is, he didn't actually have a gun. It was all bluff. He just pretended to have one in his pocket."

To demonstrate, he poked his index finger out straight, like it had turned into a revolver, and held it menacingly under his T-shirt, aimed at me.

Nothing was ever quite the same after that. I'd had enough of my criminal housemates. It wasn't fun anymore. I hadn't thought too highly of Taylor Gates to begin with, but he had shocked me by turning out to be an even more compromised and deceitful human being than I'd ever suspected, a treacherous and amoral opportunist, a genuinely scary guy who by his nature would simply continue to charm and use anyone as long as he could.

I kept busy elsewhere, came up with excuses, tried not to be obvious, but didn't hang out with them after that. Since I was the only one who wasn't shooting up, I was a natural to be left out, anyway.

One night after work, however, I didn't have my excuses ready quickly enough, and an invitation from Rudy and Jade caught me off-guard. Before I knew it, Taylor was bullying me into accepting, and since it promised to be just a quick drive, I saw no harm in letting myself be strong-armed into joining them.

We ended up waiting for hours in a north end supermarket parking lot. By the time the Mexican finally drove up and delivered, Rudy was too sleepy to drive home. That was all Taylor needed to hear. He eagerly took the wheel and set off speeding back to Seattle, eager to enjoy a glove compartment full of top quality purchases.

Taylor drove like a maniac, which was scary enough, passing cars with only a few inches of room, chasing trucks, showing off for Jade, but his fancy driving finally attracted a little too much attention. A police squad car began wailing after us and pulled us over, blue light revolving. To my horror I found myself trapped in a car with drug addicts, sitting terrified in the back seat holding Dude, knowing my friends had a glove compartment full of illegal goodies and that I was about to be arrested. I had written my last book review. I would be spending the rest of my life behind bars.

To top it off, Taylor didn't have ID or a driver's license. He and Rudy had just enough time for a rapid-fire exchange of furious, frantic whispers in the front seat. Then they both crouched down and crawled past each other, changing places to put Rudy in the driver's seat before rolling down the window. At that point, I was so scared I was on the edge of throwing up.

The officer smiled, and using a very ironic tone of voice said that he couldn't help but notice some rather suspicious movement down low in the front seat.

"I was looking for my registration papers," explained Rudy. "I thought they were in the glove compartment."

Since it was Rudy's car it made logical sense that the driver would be Rudy. They were interrupted by an all-cars alert coming through the police radio. The officer hurriedly gave Rudy the benefit of the doubt, and wrote him a quick ticket for a broken taillight. He told Rudy to drive more carefully, and dashed off to some other crime scene.

That's the only thing that kept us out of jail. That was the last night I joined them.

I still saw Rudy alone sometimes in the afternoon, especially if he was watching Dude. I'd come over to play with the dog, and Rudy would recount to me their adventures.

Though I was repelled by their behavior, I found the stories irresistible. Taylor continued to be the instigator of their various petty crimes, and controlled Rudy and Jade completely through their habits. Rudy would follow Taylor anywhere. Rudy would do whatever Taylor told him to do. Jade would provide the entertainment afterward.

Life had been kind to them so far. They had never been caught. No one had been seriously hurt. But they'd had some close calls that were heart-stopping, the daily risk of grim consequences for those who operate on the far side of the law. In the evenings after work, Rudy would pass me his bong and entertain me with harrowing tales of the trio's near-misses with the police.

Only once did their luck run out. That night Rudy went along with Taylor to see a new dealer. This guy lived in the "no drug traffic zone" on Capital Hill. When Taylor phoned him from his cell to say they'd arrived, the guy refused to let Taylor bring anyone else along with him. Rudy was left in the car. Taylor took longer than usual. While Rudy was impatiently waiting for Taylor to come back out, a white squad car pulled up beside him and blocked him in. Rudy was arrested for loitering, and taken to jail.

Though he was only behind bars for a few hours, released when the searching of his car came up with no drugs, Rudy still ended up paying for that night dearly. The court papers regarding the incident were mailed to his parents' home. His mother suspected Rudy was on drugs again, and refused to give him his inheritance from his grandfather.

Rudy was devastated. He had been counting on that windfall to pay his debts and catch up. He sank into a bleak, soul-eating depression from which he had not yet recovered, continuing to survive from day to day on the edge of being sick, desperately entrusting his weekly Unemployment money to Taylor, hoping against hope that Taylor would keep him well, pawning every possession he could pawn.

Taylor Gates was unstoppable. Rudy's brief incarceration scarcely registered on his forward momentum. One lick led to another. He robbed a little restaurant in Belltown where he used to wait tables. He burglarized a home grower's illegal basement crop of marijuana. He relieved a gay community center of their newly-installed computer system. He emptied the tills of two more grocery stores and took on his first all-night gas station.

The licks lifted his spirits. They went off like clockwork. He was good at it.

Chapter 11
Accident

About a week later I came home from the bookstore to the usual enthusiastic welcome and licking from Dude. Taylor was just leaving, dashing off a half hour late with Rudy in tow, after the two of them had diligently concocted something with brown sugar and coffee grounds that looked a lot like heroin.

I happily settled in behind my computer screen with Dude on my lap and a cup of coffee beside me. I had managed to finish several hours of intense work when I was interrupted by the sound of the door down the hall banging open and slamming shut. A moment later Dude gave a sharp bark and I looked up to find Rudy standing there in my doorway looking like an escaped victim from a zombie movie. One of his lips was bleeding, and he had a gash down one eyebrow. One cheek was scratched. One knee of his pants was torn.

"What the hell happened to you?"

I jumped to my feet in sheer urgent amazement, my mouth opening and shutting uselessly. Dude landed gracefully on the floor, circled skittering around Rudy until he was sure the situation was resolved, and then hopped into the chair behind me.

"My car," said Rudy in a daze, as though answering some question I had already asked. His little black Honda Civic was usually parked down near the corner under my window. "My poor car. It's totaled."

"It's *what?*"

"I don't have a car anymore."

He walked into the room stiffly, as though every step hurt. He looked like he'd just walked away from the scene of the accident. Slowly I began to realize he had done just that. He wiped his lip on the back of his hand. His eyes were skittish and he was trembling.

"Are you okay?" I asked stupidly, since the evidence to the contrary was right in front of my eyes.

"No, I'm not okay," he snapped. "I have just lost my car." He sank down onto my sofa. One of his hands had blood on it, and left fingerprints on the cushion.

I sat down beside him. "Are you hurt?"

"No, no, I'm fine."

"How'd you do it?" I waited for him to answer, and when he didn't, I pressed him with, "How did you manage to wreck your car?"

He hesitated. I couldn't tell whether he hadn't heard me, or was toying with the idea of lying. He sighed as he made his decision, and pushed the words out. "It wasn't me."

Either I was being thick-headed, or he wasn't telling me enough. "You mean, it wasn't your fault?"

"I mean, I wasn't driving."

"Someone else was driving your car? Who?" Two seconds later, of course, I realized there was only one guy it could have been, and we both said his name at the same time.

"Taylor."

"Why was he driving your car? He's got his own."

"Because his car was out of gas and I was in no condition to drive mine. I didn't want to go. He did."

"Go where?"

"To meet his Mexican. That guy is never on time."

"What happened?"

"We were both too high to drive, but Taylor said he could do it and I didn't stop him, that's what happened." I could tell he didn't want to talk about it, but he was too angry to be silent. "I tried to tell him, be smart, man, we've got enough for tomorrow, don't do any more, wait till you're home, but, oh no, not Taylor, he always wants to be just a little bit higher."

"He was getting high while he was driving?"

"Not high enough for Taylor." He wouldn't meet my eye. "I said, Slow down. He said, If we're late, he'll leave. I said, Doesn't matter, we've got enough for tomorrow. He said, No, we don't, because I'm going to do some more right now. And that's just what he did, the stupid fuck. So then he's going super-fast. He's flooring it, man. And he… well, shit, he nodded off," he said, almost too softly to be heard. "He missed the turn."

Two weeks later Taylor wrecked his own car exactly the same way he had wrecked Rudy's, by shooting up too much heroin and then nodding off at the wheel. He took down a signpost and nearly went off the bridge, but didn't hit anyone else and got out of the crumpled car with nothing worse than a swollen forehead.

Like Rudy's car, Taylor's big boat of a Fifties' relic was destroyed beyond repair.

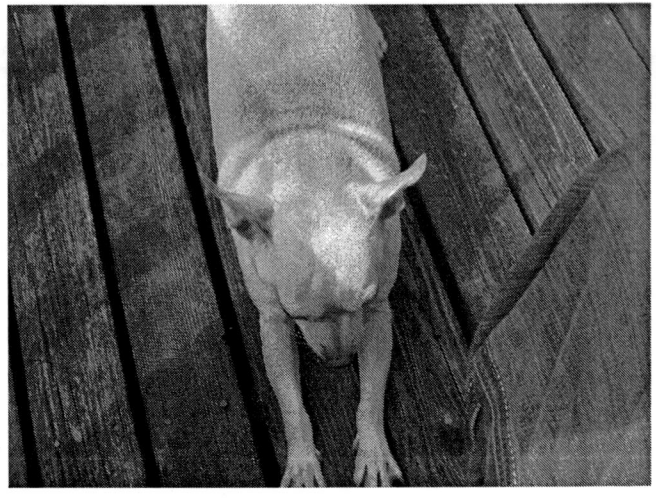

Chapter 12

A Visit from the Police

When I got home the following afternoon, Mrs Stoll was standing in the kitchen doorway, wide-eyed and waiting for me. She was wearing her familiar pink sweater of thick, bulky yarn that she'd knitted herself twenty years ago, her arms folded across her chest against the cold.

She did not look happy.

I stopped on the third step of the back staircase. It was clear Mrs Stoll had something she very much wanted to say.

"The police," she mouthed in an urgent whisper, as though the neighbors might be eavesdropping. "They were here." She gave me a moment to digest that much, and then added, "They were looking for him."

As though it would be bad luck to even mention his name, she pointed up toward the second floor, in the general direction of Taylor's apartment. "This morning they came here. They knocked on the front door. They scared me. They said they are coming back very soon. They said we have to call them the minute that man comes back here. They said if we do not call them, we will be arrested, too."

I doubted that was exactly what they'd told her, but I got the message. Helping Taylor in any way, even with silence, would be a crime. I didn't wait to hear any more. I went up the back stairs two at a time, flung open the door at the top and collided headlong with Rudy, who was standing in some kind of stupor just inside the hall door.

"Rudy, what happened? Where's Taylor? Rudy?"

He was completely out of it. He seemed to be falling asleep on his feet, teetering in a trance, as though he were listening to distant music that no one else could hear.

"Hey, man, are you all right?" He was slowly leaning forward, farther, farther, until he was almost tipping over. He righted himself with a jerk. "Rudy? Are you okay?"

"The cops are after him."

We were standing right outside Taylor's room. The sound of our voices promptly caused scratching at the door and a frustrated bark on the other side. "How did the police find out? From the Mexican?"

Rudy closed his eyes and shook his head in slow-motion. "This isn't about drugs."

He kept wobbling on his feet, teetering like he was about to fall over, until I finally just had to ask, "Rudy, are you high?"

A goofy smile of recollection rippled over his face. "I was getting depressed."

I should have realized sooner. "You shot up at a time like this?"

Dude barked again, reminding me that the hallway was no place for this conversation. I helped Rudy into his apartment, closed the door, and guided him toward the bedroom. "Why are the police after Taylor?"

He sank down on the side of the bed, like a man at sea who doesn't quite have his sea legs. "Taylor was having a cash flow problem."

"So? Nothing new in that. We all do. That's why some of us have jobs."

"So he decided to solve the problem with a little criminal activity."

"Okay, fine, I don't want to know any more."

But there was no stopping him. "He still had a key to the house he used to live in. His old landlord didn't have much, but he *did* have…"

"Stop right there. That's more than I want to know."

I couldn't help wondering if Rudy had helped him. Maybe they were in this together. I considered that Rudy and Taylor might be closer than I thought. For all I knew, they could even be lovers. "Do you know where Taylor is? Are you worried about him?"

"Taylor can take care of himself," he said. "Whatever else he does, I assure you, he knows how to take care of himself." It took Rudy a moment to gather his strength before he continued. "You must have figured out by now that Taylor can be a mean son of a bitch."

"I've seen his anger close up," I admitted. The day he thought I'd stolen his heroin was still fresh in my memory. "It wasn't a pretty sight."

"It can get pretty ugly," he agreed. "That's why I try not to annoy him, because I can't make it without him." At first I thought he was confessing that he was in love with Taylor. The thought must have showed on my face, because he sighed. "Nah, he's just my dealer. At least, he was. I don't know where I'm going to get my stuff now." He looked at me with unconcealed desperation, as though maybe, by some stroke of luck, I might have a reliable heroin connection.

"He has my money. He keeps spending it on that little bitch. That's why he can't pay his Mexican. He's fucking up, and I need him. I'm starting to get sick."

Staying out of criminal activity is smart, but ignorance is always a liability. I decided it wasn't safe for me not to know more. "Okay, I've changed my mind. Tell me. Why are the police after Taylor?"

"Because he stole he old landlord's guitar," he said patiently, spelling it out for me.

"Damn, what a stupid thing to do!"

Rudy shook his head. "Not stupid when you've got to get your hands on some money fast. He knew his old landlord's work schedule."

I had to ask. "Did you drive for him?"

I could tell by the look on his face. "The whole thing would have gone smoothly, except that some asshole neighbor recognized Taylor's car."

"But what's he going to do with a stolen guitar?"

"Pawn it, what do you think? It's already pawned. To get enough money to buy more stuff from the Mexican." Rudy sank back wearily on his bed, kicking off his slippers onto the floor. He wouldn't look me in the eye. "I oughta know. He got me to pawn it for him."

"You pawned a stolen guitar?" I didn't have to ask why he'd done such a stupid thing, because he was honest enough to admit it.

"He offered me an eight-ball. Sure, I pawned it."

"But why couldn't he do it himself?"

He was talking to his pillow now, more than he was talking to me. "Because Taylor doesn't have ID. I do." He groaned, and then added, "We drove directly from the pawn shop to the Mexican. Which was nice, except Taylor just had to start celebrating early. It was on our way back from there that he totaled his car."

"Where is he now?"

"Who knows?"

I fell asleep trying not to hear Dude whimpering down at the end of the hall, alone in Taylor's darkening apartment, scratching at the door that remained closed and locked. Did he have food? How long had he been locked in there? His whines were puppylike and frightened.

He'd spent the whole day frantically waiting for someone to come home. No one had come. He'd been forgotten, and that was something Dude didn't like at all.

Chapter 13
Dude Changes Hands

I was hugging my pillow, sound asleep. The house was dark and silent. Not a floorboard was creaking. No one was moving anywhere.

I woke up suddenly, completely disoriented, my heart beating too loudly and too fast. The only light was from the streetlamp on the corner, but it was enough. I glanced at my wrist to see what time it was, and realized that I'd forgotten my watch in the bathroom. All I could tell was that it was sometime in the middle of the night, and I could hear sharp voices barking at each other in the hall.

Taylor had come home.

I quickly got out of bed, pulled on my pants and headed for the door. As I rushed out, I found Rudy in his pajama bottoms arguing with Taylor, whose unzipped jacket made him look like he'd just come in from the night. Both of them seemed to be trying to keep their voices down. Rudy took a look in my direction and stopped whatever he was saying. Taylor took the opportunity to stick his key into the lock.

The moment his door opened, Dude burst out of confinement with a few sharp barks until Taylor swept him into his arms. What at first looked like affection was instead extreme agitation. He gripped Dude unkindly, holding his mouth shut.

"Quiet, you dumb dog!" he said through clenched teeth. "Or I'm going to strangle you." He tossed the little guy to the floor behind him, strode into his apartment, pulled open a big backpack on his bed and started frantically stuffing in a couple shirts and a hoodie. When the little dog came scurrying in after him, Taylor pushed him roughly away. "Stay out of my way, and don't you dare start barking."

Dude barked.

He swung out as though to hit him. The little dog scuttled out of reach. Taylor muttered threats and continued yanking open drawers and jerking hangers with shirts out of the closet. "I'm sick of all your barking. You're going to screw everything up. Don't piss me off."

I crouched down within licking distance and let Dude get a good taste of my face. At least, while he was licking me, he was quiet. Rudy and I hovered just outside the apartment while Taylor lunged back and forth packing his backpack and cursing up a storm, slamming things, breaking things, muttering. He grabbed keys, wallet, lighter, Swiss army knife, and various papers, and what didn't fit into his backpack he stuffed into his pockets.

Rudy had stayed quiet for as long as he could. "Please," he said, continuing some conversation I hadn't heard, "it would only take you a couple minutes."

"No more of your bullshit, Rudy," he snapped back. He refused to even look at him. All his attention was focused on the bulging backpack open on the bed, into which he was trying to squeeze the last few things he could take with him. "Can't you get that through your head? You're on your own. I can't help you anymore."

"But you could tell the Mexican…"

Taylor yanked the backpack zipper shut, slung it over his shoulder, and turned around to thrust his face up to within an inch of Rudy's. "I've already told you. He won't deal with you. You're too obvious and desperate and besides that, you're a pain in the ass. Fuck off, man. I helped you while I could. That's over."

Rudy's lower lip was trembling. "The police said we had to call them as soon as you showed up."

"Yeah? Well, I'll be out of here before they can get here." He tugged off his T-shirt over his head, threw it in the corner, pulled on a fresh one, and then buttoned up another shirt on top of that.

Dude squirmed out of my arms and galloped over to the corner where Taylor had tossed the T-shirt, snatched it up in his jaws and began beating it to death on the floor.

"The policeman said if we didn't call as soon as you showed up, we were accessories to the crime," said Rudy.

That's where I finally had enough and butted in. "Yeah, well, don't worry about that, Rudy, okay?" I said, cutting him off. "We're not making any phone calls to anyone until long after he's out of here. We're not that rotten." I surprised myself. I thought I was just thinking the words, and instead they came out of my mouth.

Taylor allowed me to have a moment's glimpse into the paranoid, criminal depths of his sad eyes. "Thanks."

Dude dropped the undershirt. It had been thoroughly flogged, and made no attempt to cause more trouble. He barked over his fallen adversary in triumph.

"Shut up, Dude!" Taylor snatched him up again into his arms, his hands just barely restraining themselves from closing around the dog's throat. "What the fuck am I going to do with this noisy dog?" He held him up in front of his face. "Dude, you're nothing but one big problem. You absolutely can't come with me." He looked around wildly, then focused on Rudy. "You're here most of the day. You take him."

"No chance," said Rudy decisively. "Princess would claw him to death."

Taylor turned to me. "Who else can I ask, man? I'll come back for him as soon as I can, I promise. You gotta help me with this."

I looked into the little dog's frightened black eyes. Big mistake. After that I couldn't deny that I'd grown to care about him. From a distance. But having the little dog visit was something completely different. Yes, he had been delightful, but just for an afternoon. Did I want the hassle and responsibility of actually living with a noisy, energetic little dog day in and day out? Of picking up his hot little turds wherever he goes?

"I don't want the Stolls to think he's my dog," I objected lamely.

"What those old coots don't know won't hurt them." Taylor laughed off my objection. "They're practically deaf. They're not going to find out. Besides, a little quality time with a dog would do you good. I'll come back and get him just as soon as I can."

"Cut it out, be real! I can't take your dog," I stammered in protest. "Babysitting him while you're making deliveries is one thing. Living with a dog 24/7 is another, man. There's no room for a dog in my life, seriously. I've got a job. I'm gone half the time."

"He'll just have to learn to live with it." Taylor's patient good humor was wearing thin. "Look, I don't have any choice. Want me to just let him loose on the street?"

"Of course not, but…"

"Well, then, take him," he said conclusively.

He thrust Dude into my arms. Suddenly I was trying to hold onto little legs that were kicking and squirming, a tongue slapping wetly at my face.

"I'll come back for him as soon as I can. He won't be any trouble." I tried to continue protesting, but no words came out. "Thanks, man. Seriously, it'll be fine, you'll see. I gotta get out of here."

He hugged the dog and me together, for a moment pulling us both up against his hot, panting body. He adjusted the straps of his backpack across his chest.

"I promise you, as soon as I can I'll be back and take him off your hands." Then he was gone, dashing down the back stairs into the dark.

Chapter 14
Disappearing Dog

That first night together was a rocky one.

After taking him on a long walk to the supermarket for kibble and dog treats and a couple cans of wet food, we arrived home somewhat bushed. I took off my shoes the minute we shuffled in the door, eased my weary body into the recliner, and was delighted to have Dude jump nonchalantly into my lap, turn around in a circle, and settle down comfortably for a little siesta on top of me as though we had always lived together.

An hour later my eyes snapped open. I struggled back to consciousness after an unexpected, unplanned nap. Dude was nowhere to be seen. Unperturbed at first, I was brewing a cup of coffee in my tiny kitchenette when it occurred to me that Dude was being very quiet.

Not until then did I realize that I didn't know exactly where he was. A frantic search checking every hiding place in my apartment revealed nothing. He wasn't there. He was no longer in my apartment – I could see that my apartment door was wide open and that wasn't all, so was the door at the end of the hall. Wide open! An invitation to disaster! Dude could be anywhere. He could be outside. He could be next door. He could be in the street.

I flung myself down the outside stairs like a lunatic, calling his name as loudly as I dared at that late hour and dashing about in all directions. "Dude! Dude, where are you? Get over here!" No dog barked in response. No little Chihuahua came scurrying toward me out of the bushes. When I had circled our block twice frantically shouting his name, I sat down on the back stairs and to my great embarrassment began to cry. How quickly I had bungled my stewardship of that helpless little dog!

All I could do was hope that he'd be able to find his way back home when he finally got hungry. I trudged sadly back up the stairs, turned on the back porch light as a hopeful beacon into the rapidly approaching night. I also left on the hall light. I propped open my door, and used the rubber doorstop to keep open the door at the end of the hall.

Then all I could do was stiffly sit waiting for him, too distracted to concentrate on my reading, straining to hear the slightest sound.

The hours dragged by with no sign of Dude. I could hardly believe I had mismanaged things so tragically. Utterly miserable, I decided to go to bed leaving the door to my apartment wide open in hopes of his returning home. Unconsciousness sounded like an utter relief from a long night of dreading. I brushed my teeth, took out my contact lenses, changed into fresh underwear. Approaching the bed, which was more rumpled than I remembered, I flung back the blankets to slide inside.

Dude was under the covers. He had burrowed down to the foot of the bed, and was curled up into a warm, furry ball, looking up at me with his huge, black eyes.

"Are you kidding me? You were here the whole time!"

At first I was actually angry. I'd wasted my entire evening in a miserable frenzy. But my anger was soon blown away by my sheer, overpowering relief.

"So you went to bed without me, huh? I hope you don't think you're going to share my bed."

He looked up at me with those big, bulging eyes, so full of emotion. Oh-oh. That was exactly what he thought. My objections were defeated before they could even be stated. It was no longer my bed. It had become *our* bed. We would be sharing the bed from now on…

Chapter 15
Eviction Notice

The next day I was a zombie at the bookstore from lack of sleep. I wasn't the only one.

When I got home that afternoon, climbed to the top of the back staircase, and entered the second floor hallway, Mrs Stoll was just huffing up the polished wooden steps of the inner staircase. I could see that the wear and tear of so much disturbance was starting to show on her face. Last night I had heard her slippers come up the inside staircase moments after Taylor left, and glimpsed the ray of her flashlight as she quietly knocked at Taylor's door to see if he had returned. I doubted she was ever able to get back to sleep after that kind of night.

Today she was looking more like a fragile senior, her back less straight, her gray hair less perfectly bunned. She gave me a brisk greeting as her heavy, uncomfortable shoes pounded up the last stair to stop outside Taylor's apartment, where she proceeded to tape an official looking document onto Taylor's door.

"There will be no more police at this house," said Mrs Stoll firmly. "The police have visited us for the last time. This is official. My nephew is a lawyer. Mister Taylor is evicted. We will find new tenant."

As soon as she returned downstairs, I dashed to my own apartment, opened the door quickly before Dude could start barking, and gave him enough treats to keep him quiet.

Her prediction that she was through with the police turned out to be untrue.

When the bus dropped me off at home the following night after work, I could see two white police cars parked in front of the house. As I hurried across the street from the bus stop, I was just in time to glimpse two policemen saying goodbye to Mrs Stoll on the front porch.

They glanced at me curiously as they passed me on the sidewalk heading back to their cars. Mrs Stoll was waiting for me on the front porch. She was wearing an apron and clutching a dish towel in one hand.

"You will be happy to know they have caught that bad man at the train station," she said in greeting, stopping me from proceeding around the house to the back staircase. "In his wallet he had a one-way ticket to Portland. But he did not escape. Now they will take him to jail. The police came here to search his room. They say he is wanted for robbery, but they did not find what they were looking for."

Of course, they didn't – because the guitar was in a pawn shop in Puyallup. The whole thing was like watching a true crime documentary on television. Unfortunately, I was on the wrong side of the camera.

I was awakened sometime around midnight by knocking at my door. I quickly scrambled out of bed and pulled on the trunks I'd dropped on the floor last night. By the light from the streetlamp in the alley, I could see a curly tail briefly exposed by the blankets I'd flung back. Dude burrowed deeper under the covers. I only hoped whoever was knocking wouldn't cause him to erupt into a loud volley of barking.

Waking up Mrs Stoll would not be a good idea.

I released the lock and opened the door just wide enough to see Jade, looking worried and cold and far too young. Her tight blue jeans clung to her legs like skin, emphasizing how skinny she was. Her faded denim jacket didn't look anywhere near warm enough.

"I'm sorry it's so late..." I quickly swung the door open wider so she could come inside. Without hesitation she hugged me, ignored the fact that I was only wearing my underwear, and held on longer than I expected with a grip that felt desperate. "Taylor hasn't called me all day. I'm so scared. I had to wait till my Dad went to bed tonight. I just wanted to know if you'd heard from him."

I toyed with not telling her what had happened. Knowing wouldn't make it any easier on her. "Well, you know, actually..." But I didn't have the energy to fabricate a lie. The way she was looking up at me, I couldn't tell her anything but the truth.

"They caught him."

She whimpered. "Where?"

"In the train station."

She wrinkled her brow in confusion. "The train station...?"

"He'd just bought a ticket to Portland."

Her crying was soundless and gut-wrenching and completely ambiguous: although at first I thought she was grieving for him being in the hands of the police, I began to suspect she was also weeping out of sheer personal fear, because she would have no fix tomorrow. The cornerstone of her habit had just been removed. She'd be forced to either go into the terrors of withdrawal, or else take her chances scoring downtown from strangers on the street.

"That's not all. He's been evicted."

I immediately regretted telling her that. It was one straw too many. It seemed to age her, changing her into a weary, little old lady. "We may never see him again."

"I doubt that. He's crazy about you. You could never get away from him, even if you wanted to."

A sudden look of urgency animated her pale face. "What about Dude? What's going to happen to him?" To answer that, I led her into the bedroom and pointed toward a lump in the blankets.

The lump moved.

A black nose emerged from underneath the rustling bedspread. One sniff, he recognized her, and out he charged. With his tail frantically wagging, she swept him into her arms, where he squirmed and strained to lick as much of her face as he could.

We looked up the case online in the King County jail register. Taylor Gates would be serving one week.

"I don't suppose you could take Dude for a few days?" I asked her hopefully.

"My father would kill me."

When she was composed enough to leave, we hugged briefly in the doorway. I wrote down my phone number on a post-it, which she crammed into her jeans' pocket as she tiptoed down the second floor hallway toward the door to the outside stairs.

When I drew back the covers to slide back into bed, I found Dude stretched out in the middle, taking up far more room than any little dog should.

"Excuse me, would you mind moving over?"

He gave a reluctant whimper as I nudged him to one side, then promptly crawled in a circle under the covers and plopped himself down against my tummy, a hot, furry little water-bottle of heat and affection.

Two days later the sentence for Taylor Gates was commuted, when they discovered that he had broken his parole, to ninety days. For three months, Dude would have no other home but my apartment.

Three months for a cat person to live with a Chihuahua…

Chapter 16
What You Need Is More Licking

When I came home from work the next day, I found the door to Taylor's apartment open, all the lights on inside, and the Stolls busily cleaning. The place reeked of disinfectant. Mr Stoll, with rolled-up sleeves and suspenders, was down on his knees in the corner, hammering at the baseboard. Mrs Stoll, in apron and kerchief, had the vacuum cleaner on one side and a huge, black garbage bag open on the other, into which she was folding and packing a heap of Taylor's shirts.

The apartment around them was as much of a pig sty as I remembered. Candy wrappers littered the floor, along with shoes, bongs, empty pop cans, unwashed underwear and an old bag of potato chips. Glass pipes and cocaine-crusted razor blades lay on the not-so-polished top of the coffee table, beside an ashtray overflowing with cigarette butts. T-shirts and jeans had been flung wildly about the room, clothes Taylor had considered taking with him and rejected at the last minute. Little bits of paper with phone numbers were taped to his mirror.

"What a nightmare," I had to comment.

"We are moving all his things down to the basement." She leaned toward me, and spoke softer. "There are things here that we do not know what they are for. And we do not want to know."

I wondered what needles and pipes and sex toys they'd stumbled on. The harsh contrast between the conservative Lutheran orderliness of the elderly German couple and the dealer's drug paraphernalia-littered chaos made me interfere.

"Here, why don't you let me take care of this?" I said, helping Mrs Stoll up onto her feet. "Don't wear yourselves out with this mess. Tomorrow's my day off, and I'll get it all packed up in a couple hours."

"We could not let you."

"I don't mind at all. Please…"

If I had hoped for a reward, the look of sheer relief on her face was more than enough.

"What a dear man you are," she said as though she sincerely meant it. "Well then, here's the key." She pressed it into my palm.

I quickly developed a habit of hurrying home after work. I would rush out of the bookstore to catch the first bus heading in my direction. I did this partly out of fear that Dude might have gotten into some mischief – he had already scattered my undershorts and socks throughout the house, ripped a cardboard toilet paper tube to smithereens, and chewed up an empty plastic yogurt container into a dozen jagged bits and pieces – and partly, I have to admit, in a growing, unexpected, hard-to-acknowledge eagerness to enjoy the company of my little four-footed pal.

Every evening at home now was studded with comic, heartwarming moments. He seemed to look forward to my company as much as I did his. Not the least of our pleasures turned out to be sleeping together.

I had a habit of frequently going to bed early. Sometimes, if I was lonely or sad, I would enjoy the option of simply checking out for the rest of the night. Why endure consciousness when you didn't have to? And now early bedtime meant affectionate companionship. Dude and I were both curled up under the covers at nine o'clock that night, with the window open on the refreshing night breeze.

Maybe in my sleep I heard someone knocking at my door around ten o'clock, but I don't remember it. I just heard Dude growling. I blinked open my eyes and discovered someone standing in my bedroom over my bed. I clawed at the bedside lamp and luckily hit the button, blinding both myself and the intruder with too much light.

"Don't be afraid," said Rudy. "Please, don't think bad things. I knocked first."

"I didn't hear you. I was asleep."

"I don't usually barge into people's houses in the night. I was just hurting and depressed and couldn't stand to be alone anymore. I didn't hook up with anyone on the street today. I'm having a very hard night."

"Sorry to hear that, buddy." I relaxed a little.

"Please, would you mind just letting me get into bed with you?"

I could hardly believe my ears. He's not unattractive, quite the opposite, in a scrawny, scruffy way he's a very appealing man, but I didn't want sexual entanglements with anyone right now in my life, no matter how charming. Those years of desperate needing were happily behind me. Sexual attraction now seemed more like hormone-induced irrational behavior. How uncomplicated life was without it!

Before I could tell him any of this, he dropped his bathrobe to the floor, drew back the covers and slipped into bed with me.

He didn't seem to realize Dude was in the bed, too, until the little dog came scrambling up and caught him by surprise planting a big wet lick across his mouth. The shock of it made Rudy unexpectedly laugh. It sounded like he hadn't laughed in a long time.

"Dude always knows what you need," I said. "Dude thinks you need more licking."

Dude curled up into a warm, round lump of fur nestled between us.

"Thanks. I couldn't take being alone anymore. See, I'm being good. But at least I'm not alone. I had to go without tonight. Some days I can't find anyone to sell me stuff. Some days they sell you crap. Some days you run out of money. It's so hard to score with Taylor gone. Sometimes I get so depressed that I start thinking about… well, you know."

I turned out the light.

Sometime during the night, Rudy took hold of my hand.

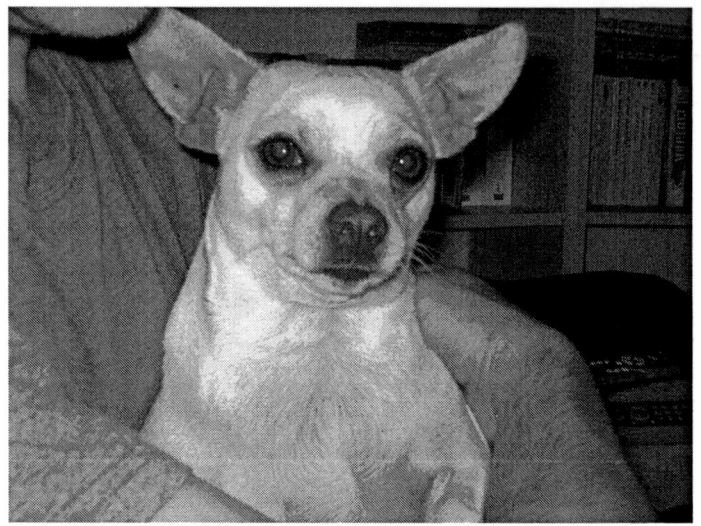

PART TWO

Chapter 17
The Good That Evil Makes

The furniture and rugs in Taylor's apartment were too stained and damaged to reuse. The project of cleaning and painting and refurnishing the little cluster of rooms at the end of the hall occupied Mr Stoll for weeks. He didn't seem to mind. Sometimes he actually whistled while he sanded and hammered and painted. He was a shy, quiet little guy who always wore suspenders, had a shy, hesitant smile, and kept to himself. I never got to know him much, but I got the feeling he might be bullied a bit by the indomitable Mrs Stoll. I often heard him down at the end of the hall, cheerfully erasing the previous occupant from our lives. There was rapidly no trace remaining of Taylor Gates.

Except that I was left with his dog.

I had sometimes imagined owning a dog. But it had always been located some time in the far, far future, when I had retired and had too much time on my hands, when I wouldn't be leaving him locked up at home alone all day long while I put in my work shifts.

I certainly never wanted a Chihuahua, and never asked to be this particular Chihuahua's owner. The thought never crossed my mind. By nature I was much more inclined to cats and their nonchalant co-existence, their self-sufficiency, inner peace, and disdain for excessive emotional displays.

Princess, the beautiful and grumpy neighbor cat, had taken to wandering the hall, and rather than have her constantly disrupting me by meowing outside my door, I'd started leaving my door slightly ajar.

She would bump open my front door, and make me aware of her presence by brushing past my leg and then back again, rubbing up against my ankles to get my attention. She did her best to ignore the bothersome little dog who tactfully steered clear of her. She quietly hated him. It wouldn't be long before Princess began making her distinctive meow, an unpleasant screech in a minor key which sounded more like the wail of a mortally wounded sheep. Then she would walk back out of my apartment, as though I didn't exist.

It wouldn't be long before she returned, dissatisfied with my performance but giving me another chance. She would demand to be fed as though it were her divine right, imperiously complaining to me about how hungry she was, demanding that I go next door and spoon a hearty portion of wet cat food into her bowl immediately, since Rudy, her silly, forgetful human being, was not complying with his duty.

Knowing how much Dude annoyed her, I left him in my apartment, closed the door behind me, and obediently followed Princess as commanded out into the hall, where I noticed Rudy's door was open.

"Rudy?"

He wasn't inside. Turning around, I disappointed Princess by going back out again, and down to the television room where more channels were available. She quickly bolted ahead of me, trotting over to where Rudy, in checkered pajama bottoms and a yellowing T-shirt, was slumped in the armchair in front of a rerun of *The Sopranos*. She did her leg-rubbing best to rouse him into feeding her.

Rudy didn't hear her. Like Princess, her owner had started spending most of his time asleep.

Rudy was a changed man. Without Taylor, his addiction had become desperate. Impulsively one weekend, out of money and facing withdrawal, he'd said goodbye to me, asked me to take care of Princess, and committed himself to a detox program. That didn't last long. The stringent rules and miserly painkiller distribution caused him to run away from the facility that very night. He had withdrawn a bit after that, embarrassed by his failure, and since I'd had my hands more than full with Dude, we had lost touch. That day, as I helped him back upstairs, I finally asked him.

"You're so sleepy all the time. Are you okay?"

"You know me, I'm a night owl," he answered glibly, nimbly avoiding the question, but a moment later at the top of the stairs he surprised me by asking, "Do I seem any different?"

"Yeah. A lot sleepier."

"It's the drug."

"You found a new dealer?"

"Nope. I found a new drug."

That's when he told me what he'd done. As he spooned a glop of cat food into Princess's bowl, he surprised me by saying, "It was too hard without Taylor. I quit, man. I'm on methadone now."

His AIDS case manager had placed an urgent call to a methadone program, and succeeded in getting him registered in a clinic where the usual waiting time was six months. Rudy was allowed to begin treatment immediately.

It was a huge turning point. He *had* to do something. It was too hard to get regular, reliable heroin. Fake stuff, cut with just about everything and reduced to uselessness, left him hurting and cost just as much as decent stuff. City-wide outages were frequent. Arrests were inevitable. He lived perpetually on the edge of being physically miserable.

Methadone was free and constantly available.

Coincidentally, on the day of his first dose, Rudy Flowers got a big helping hand from the Seattle Police Department. Five squad cars converged that night on the Eastlake Motel in a surprise sting and arrested the Mexican. Suddenly, for a day or two, no one in the north end had anything to sell. Rudy had no alternative – it was methadone or nothing. By the time heroin was available again and a new Mexican had taken the old one's place, the methadone had started to satisfy him.

It was the end of an era.

Rudy left the house early every morning now to bus to the methadone clinic. Then he would come home and fall asleep in front of the television, sometimes in his room, sometimes downstairs, which was where I would find him when Princess became too annoying.

One day at a time, Rudy left his old habit behind.

Though he now had a tendency to doze off in day-swallowing naps, he had finally escaped from the crippling addiction that had enslaved him to Taylor Gates.

Chapter 18
Evil Shower, Guilty Underwear

Slowly Dude and I grew to know each other. As June heated up into July, and July sizzled and blistered into August, a strange and wonderful understanding blossomed between us.

To my surprise, our primary language was not words, but games. Dude communicated his happiness and his interconnectedness with everything around him in a variety of repeatable games and rites. As I learned to pay attention to him, he taught them to me.

Every morning, for instance, began with a routine I thought of as my crotch-confirmation. I would wake up first. I quickly became busy at my computer in the writing room. That's where he would find me. He'd make his way across the tiny kitchen, his toe nails clicking on the linoleum tiles like little castanets, announcing his arrival long before his big ears appeared in the doorway of my writing room.

In he would trot, circle around my swivel chair, duck under my writing table, and stick his nose in my crotch. There he would sniff audibly, bumping his nose up against my scrotum, confirming that I really was who I appeared to be. The unique and particular smell of my groin was my one distinguishing, defining trait. Only one man's groin smelled exactly like that.

Similarly, our breakfast ritual was one of the day's dependable and repeatable pleasures.

Every morning he would watch until he saw the yogurt container and spoon in my hand. No matter how quietly done, he would always hear the seal over the yogurt being peeled back. He would come charging into the little kitchen, come skidding to a halt at my feet, and watch me intently as I spooned in some raspberry jam, and stirred it into the yogurt thoroughly. The sight never failed to launch him toward the armchair, where he knew I would settle down for breakfast. To convince me of his willingness to participate in that breakfast, Dude would do his dance.

Rapidly lunging back and forth from one armrest to the other, hopping from right to left like the seating cushion had become red hot, his little legs would tap their way through some complex Mexican folk dance known only to him, with his neck and head raised in an overwhelming surge of readiness and impatience and sheer availability. Caught up in the feverish excitement of anticipation, he would become the very picture of eagerness.

The moment I sank down into the armchair, he would bound out from behind me to land in my lap, his eyes fixed on the yogurt container. He would wait like a gentleman for the first spoonful of yogurt to be plopped down on the endtable beside me, and then he would lunge, tongue first, into an orgy of noisy, sloppy lapping.

Every morning we played the same game when I took my shower. There would be no sign of him when I turned on the water. If he was anywhere nearby, he would leave. He made it clear that he didn't like that drumming, splattering hissing sound. He did not savor one bit the concept of a drenching.

As soon as I turned off the water, however, he would slip boldly into the bathroom, stealthily approaching my discarded undershorts. Then, when I drew aside the shower curtain, I would find him standing vigilantly, like a conqueror, in the middle of the bathroom rug, my undershorts held down with one valiant paw.

He always whimpered. He seemed to regret that I had just washed away all my odors. He wasn't sure it was still me. He would rush up to the bathtub, rear up onto his hind legs, and sniff my groin, where hopefully not all the smell had been perfumed away with soap. Once he was sure that I was really me, he would take justice into his own paws. He would lunge on my guilty undershorts, grip them in his jaws and while making his fiercest growls, whack them back and forth on the floor, teaching them a lesson they would never forget.

It was merciless, unapologetic retribution. In some fierce world of dog values, my undershorts deserved it.

Dude blithely violated many dog stereotypes.

Take fetching. I assumed that Dude had the classic instincts of all dogs, that he wouldn't need special coaching to know how to fetch. The master threw something, and the dog brought it back. It was ancient, time-tested. It was part of our primeval arrangement with the canine race.

Like any good dog, Dude seemed to innately understand the concept of chasing a Frisbee. He was excited. He was eager. His tongue was lolling out. His eyes appeared to be laughing. He had figured out that we were there in the park to play. He was waiting for me to throw it. He was off his halter, free of the leash, unrestrained.

I would send the Frisbee sailing out across the weedless green lawn of the little park, and at the same time, I would cry, "Fetch!"

Off he would go! His little legs scampering as fast as he could, eagerly lunging headlong, for a thrilling moment it would look almost as though he finally got the idea, he was really chasing the Frisbee, that this time the timeless instinct to pursue and capture had kicked in, he was going to leap up and snag it.

But no, this little dog had a short attention span and Frisbees weren't all that interesting. Before galloping very far Dude became so intoxicated with the sheer joy of running that he would go dashing merrily off in some completely other direction, and the Frisbee would sail away forgotten.

He felt no urge to chase a Frisbee. The happiness was in running. Running he loved to do. It had nothing to do with the silly object I couldn't seem to hang onto, that kept sailing off into the air.

That wasn't the only thing that little dog refused to learn.

There was no curbing his perpetual instinct to be licking me. Was it to show affection? Was it to monitor my food intake? I never knew for sure. It was more than a habit, it seemed to be ingrained and unstoppable. My training attempts were making no progress. I could see that sooner or later I would have to compromise.

Finally I decided to sacrifice one body part. There I would allow him do what his nature drove him to do. Not on the lips. Not on the groin. From now on Dude would be allowed to lick me in only one place.

On the nose.

As long as he restricted his wet affection to my nose, I would close my eyes and let that powerful tongue of his have its way.

It was all a matter of accommodation.

I tried to be the most understanding human partner I could be. I tried to read his signals. I never bullied him. I regretted that I had to leave him alone during the workday, but fortunately most of my shifts were only five hours long.

Every evening we walked a mile to the supermarket for groceries. He would tug me along eagerly, his nose to the ground, reading messages in the grass that I couldn't smell, leaving a few messages himself on the corners of buildings, on trees and telephone poles and fire hydrants. He did this at least once every block, all the way there, long after he'd run out of urine, inspecting anything unusual on the sidewalk, sniffing any flowers along the parking strips, and tugging me along behind him tirelessly.

Until he spotted a dog.

One sight of another pooch, across the street or on the sidewalk ahead of us, and Dude would go berserk. He became possessed. He changed into another animal. He literally left all his training and good behavior behind, came completely unglued and snapped into an alternate Dude who was determined to sound the alarm, who would not be silenced until the truth was heard, louder and louder as though he had lost his mind. Flinging himself savagely toward the other dog, again and again, his repeated lunges on the leash would transform him into a noisy, four-footed top, spinning in the grips of a demon.

Why? Was he afraid of other dogs? Was he making a lot of racket in an attempt to scare them away? Sometimes I thought it was the little dog's compensation. Sometimes I thought Dude believed he owned me, and when he saw another dog on the sidewalk he was warning that dog not to even *think* about approaching me. I was taken, I was guarded, and he wouldn't put up with any funny business.

Or did it come from some terrifying experience when he was young? How I wished I could penetrate the mystery of Dude's past. I would never know the world he came from. I had only one clue – across the bridge of his nose was a little crooked line about a quarter of an inch long that looked like someone wrote on Dude with a ballpoint pen.

On closer inspection, you could see it was not ink. It was a scar. One day when he was just a puppy Dude was clawed across the face.

The thing about dogs is that we *think* we know what goes on in their minds, but we can never know for sure. Dogs have a look that seems to be laughing, but is it? Dogs seem to be kissing us, or are they just tasting our lips to see what we've been eating? All we can do is make theories about them, and test the theories to see if they seem to answer the question of what is actually transpiring in the canine mind.

Stories from the dog's point of view, novels and movies where dogs think or talk, began to seem silly and annoying. They didn't show respect for what couldn't be known.

The closer I got to Dude, the more I realized that in our special, temporary friendship we both were operating on a system of blind trust. We both believed that the other wouldn't harm us. I knew when he took my fingers into his jaws and closed his teeth on them, that he wouldn't close all the way, that he would never hurt me on purpose. I liked to think that he knew the same.

Those were only a few of the many dog mysteries with which I now lived daily. What was Dude afraid of when he saw me go into the shower? Why did he try to "kill" my undershorts? Why did he go ballistic when he saw another dog? What exactly was he doing when he snatched up one of my socks and ran triumphantly across the apartment with it in his mouth?

Our endless human fascination with the canine race has something profound to do with the trust of believing in their love, combined with the perpetual uncertainty of never knowing for sure what they're thinking.

Chapter 19
How Dogs Are Not Cats

It was a brave new world, and I was a blundering, inexperienced player, an ignorant dog owner discovering through trial and error all the ways dogs were not cats.

Once, long ago in my remote childhood, there had been a dog in my life, but I remembered very little about him. Sparky was a small, frisky Airedale, and though he was the family dog, he was mostly my mother's concern. I bonded more with our childhood cat, Mary.

My brother and I were rough with our pets. We were little monsters without meaning to be. Never actually intending her harm, we thought it was great fun to lock Mary in drawers and boxes, or to drop Mary down the laundry chute onto a pile of clothes. Only after being involved as an adult in several long-term relationships with cats had the whole concept of respectful human/animal communication penetrated my thick *homo sapiens* skull.

Buddy and I lived together as housemates, not as master and cat. I was Buddy's door-opener and can-opener, and otherwise we were equals. I never ordered him around. I tried to understand his concerns. I gave him the happiest life possible.

He liked to eat at the same level that I ate, and so his bowls were on the kitchen drainboard, not on the floor. How that single concession scandalized my friends! But I never bullied him. I never said what he could do and couldn't do. That way he could be himself, and I could see who he really was. Whenever I was sick, for instance, Buddy never left my bed. He guarded me and comforted me and kept me warm. Buddy blamed my suitcase every time I went on a trip. All he had to do was see it lying open on the bed, airing out before packing, and he would quickly drench it in urine.

After his death, just looking at an open suitcase would bring me to tears.

Meanwhile I was trying to I understand this new creature who had moved in with me. Dogs were clearly not cats, I was smart enough to see they were two vastly different experiences, and it had taken me about twenty years to learn enough about cats to live well with one. How would I ever manage to understand this goofy dog?

Understanding comes from knowledge. That's what I was lacking. Because of my inexperience with dogs in general and total ignorance of Chihuahuas in particular, hoping to learn how to distinguish which traits were simply doggish, and which were specifically Chihuahuan, as a bookseller, I naturally turned to the resource I knew and loved best.

At the bookstore I zeroed in on Alexandra Horowitz's *Inside of a Dog*. I immediately bought a copy, took it home, and read through the first ninety pages. She clearly loved dogs, and seemed to genuinely understand them. The chapter on smell alone was eye-opening. Two days later I bought a copy of *The Chihuahua Handbook* by Dr. Caroline Coile, which kept me up half the night reading all the sidebars and enjoying all the pictures. Information, that was what I needed, because knowledge would surely lead to some kind of understanding. It could! it could! I was going to understand this little guy. I kept hoping for an epiphany, a sudden blaze of wisdom that would illuminate canine mentality.

Momentarily closing J. R. Ackerley's delightful *My Dog Tulip* in order to shift my legs before they fell asleep, I accidentally woke Dude from his afternoon snooze in my lap.

He wasn't the only one sleeping. I was starting to worry about Rudy, who since he'd started his methadone treatment did little but sleep all day. Dude could tell I was restless and jumped down to the floor. As I headed out of the apartment, he scampered along after me and looked at me with big, sad eyes when I closed the door on him. I didn't want him downstairs. I thought it might be smarter to keep him out of the way of Mrs Stoll.

Descending the inner staircase as quietly as I could, trying not to make the old stairs squeak too badly, I stepped into the television room. There was no sign of the elderly couple, but Rudy was still sleeping. It was two o'clock on a late summer afternoon. He'd been dozing here all day, slumped over in the recliner while the television proceeded merrily along without him, laughing and cheering its way through some inane game show.

I was tempted to wake him, but didn't. I'd been trying to make sure he ate better. He'd gained a few pounds, didn't look quite so skeletal. Now that he was on the methadone program, I didn't have to worry about his drug habit devouring his weekly check.

His eyes fluttered open. "What time is it?"

When I told him, he groaned. He tried to get up and seemed to be having trouble, so I took his arm and hauled him up out of the armchair, steering him across the Oriental carpet toward the staircase, walking up the stairs close behind him to make sure he didn't fall. Closing the door of his apartment behind us, I settled him limply into his armchair and slid his shoes off his feet.

Princess strolled into the room, regarded me suspiciously as I headed for the door, and then decided to honor Rudy with her company by bounding up into his lap, where she curled up smugly into a ball of well-brushed fur.

We found ourselves accidentally becoming a family. A lonely bookseller, a methadone-zonked addict, an annoyed cat, and a drug dealer's dog. The four of us had become unintentional housemates.

It could so easily have been a tragedy. It had all the telltale ingredients for a story with a very sad outcome. Instead Dude had passed easily from Taylor's hands into mine and got himself a real chance at happiness.

The two of us discovered that we could live together peacefully, that a lonely cat person and a highly energized Chihuahua, the unlikeliest of housemates, could somehow cohabit without driving each other crazy.

Too good to be true? You could say that. I suddenly found myself embarassingly happy – too happy, actually. Real people can't bear to stay happy for long. Sooner or later someone would have to pay the price. Sooner or later poor, sleepy Rudy was going to slip back into his heroin addiction. Sooner or later, Taylor would come back to claim his dog, and I would have to say goodbye to Dude.

That was how the world worked. Everyone knew there was more grief than happiness.

But because it was doomed not to last, every day was especially precious, every hour spent with Dude became a particular delight. He was not my dog, I had to keep reminding myself. I did not own him. He belonged to Taylor. I was just a babysitter. Babysitters are left behind. At any moment, my cherished little friend could be taken away from me.

Sooner or later I would lose him.

Chapter 20

No Dogs Allowed (Part 1)

The letter was a shock: simple and ugly and perfectly clear. At first I was thoroughly confused to get a stamped letter from the woman who lived downstairs, but as the icy tone of the words slowly chilled me, I realized she was just covering her legal bases. Once again, her nephew, the lawyer, had been advising her how to proceed. Mrs Stoll was writing to me so that her words would be permanent. There weren't many. The entire letter consisted of two sentences. She was formally reaffirming what my lease already clarified, that only cats were allowed in her three upstairs rental units.

Dogs were prohibited.

I dropped into a chair.

Breathe, I thought. I took a couple deep breaths. I had known all along it was against the rules. There has to be a way around this. Maybe because he was no bigger than a cat, she would be reasonable. I simply assumed it would be fine, that since Rudy had the right to have Princess, Dude would be just as permitted.

I could only stare at her letter in horror, reading it over and over again, memorizing the contents without trying to, frantically trying to think of a way out.

The following evening there was a firm, crisp knocking at my door.

Luckily I heard her heavy footsteps coming up the inner staircase first, so by the time she knocked I had quickly pushed back my chair, clicked on Save, scooped up Dude off the armchair beside me and rushed him into the bedroom, where I lifted the covers and popped him under them. "Please, stay put and don't bark." At this touchy time, the less Mrs Stoll saw of him the better. Then I took a deep breath, and opened the door.

"I want to make sure you have no questions about my letter," she said, standing clearly on her side of the threshold into my apartment. She had obviously knocked on my door fully prepared for my resistance, and ready to deal with it. "In this house there will be no dogs."

"No dogs?" I could only repeat her words in a mournful echo. I scrambled for the right thing to say, swallowing my exasperation. I tried not to show how annoyed I was at the sheer lunacy of the policy. "Not even very little dogs that are smaller than cats?"

"It is clearly in your lease," she said with patient, unwavering sternness. "Cats are allowed, dogs are not."

"I'm afraid I didn't read my lease," I confessed, trying to keep the fear out of my voice. Surely this woman didn't expect me to get rid of the delightful little dog who was bringing me so much joy. Surely she wouldn't enforce such insanity!

I tried to nudge the conversation along to a tolerant conclusion so I could get back to work. "Sincerely, I never intended to have a dog. I didn't plan it. But this little guy all of a sudden didn't have a home. And now he shares mine. I mean, he's become my friend. He loves me. I can't just phone the Humane Society and say, 'Come over and pick him up.'"

"You signed the lease but did not read it," she summarized. "I am afraid that is a very careless thing to do."

"But he's so small. He's smaller than Princess, that's for sure."

"I allow Mr Rudy to have his Princess, because that is what we have agreed upon in our lease. A cat is one thing and a dog is another."

"But someday the owner will be coming back for this little dog."

"And when is this?"

"Well, I'm not sure. It could be any week now…"

"I'm sorry, no dogs are allowed here." She smiled sadly. "This one must go."

Those were her last words as she turned and shuffled out of the room, pulling the door closed behind her.

I was so miserable I couldn't eat, I couldn't read, I couldn't type a civilized sentence. The dreadful idea of being forced to get rid of Dude lurked behind every thought. I couldn't betray him. It was too late for deserting him. Somewhere in my heart I had made a commitment, and I would have to live up to it.

We were a team now.

Which left me with only one alternative, so physically exhausting I couldn't bear to even consider it – I would have to move again! Finally I sat down at my desk and wrote:

Dear Mr and Mrs Stoll,

I am very sorry to have broken your rule about dogs. I broke it without knowing. My cat died in March. I moved to your house to get away from sad memories. Since then I've lived without a pet. I had no intention of getting a dog. I only volunteered to keep this Chihuahua for a week.

I am pleading with you to make an exception to the no-dogs rule. He weighs ten pounds, less than Princess and he's smaller. He's well-trained and housebroken. He's short-haired and has no odor and has caused no damage. He doesn't disturb the neighbors with barking. He only does his business in the little triangle of grass at the end of the yard by the alley. He's so small he's hardly a dog at all.

I turned HIV-positive a year before moving here. This month on my quarterly visit to the doctor I received the best health report I've ever received. My immune system is no longer dangerously dwindling. My viral load has become undetectable. I credit much of my health surge to the joy I get from little Dude. He's always happy to see me, and constantly makes me laugh.

I enjoy living here. I have tried to be a very cooperative and low-maintenance occupant. It would be a huge strain on my health to move. I sincerely hope that you value a quiet, responsible tenant enough to make an exception to the cats-only rule. I would be very, very grateful. For someone so tiny, he contributes so much to my life.

I tiptoed down the inner staircase, and slid it under the door. No response. The next day I waited for her knock, but it never came. Not until the following afternoon when I came home from work did I find a phone message waiting for me. It was very brief. Since the dog was so very, very small, the Stolls had decided to make a special exception.

Dude could stay.

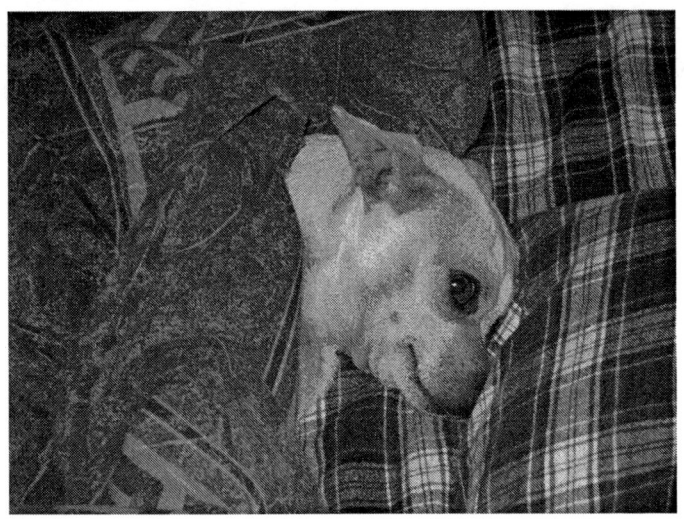

Chapter 21
No Dogs Allowed (Part 2)

That was the beginning of everything going wrong.

The landlord problem was resolved happily enough but trouble wasn't through with us by a long shot. It came back again, on a day that began so delightfully that the farthest thing from my mind was a confrontation.

The last, long sunny days of August had come to an end. With September, as the first trees began changing color, it was increasingly obvious that over the summer I had changed, too. All my resistance had crumbled. I had completely fallen in love with a superb and truly delightful little being. As a result I was living a new life of optimism and laughter. The cloud of mourning and solitude that had been hanging over me had dissolved upon his arrival in my life.

Jacob noticed the change in me even before I saw it myself. He propped up his bicycle outside my door in the hallway, even though Mrs Stoll had told him repeatedly that it was not allowed. He wasn't wearing enough clothes, making the most of the last of the nice weather.

"You're smiling all the time. It's almost annoying," he complained. "What's gotten into you? Are you on drugs?" He quickly took all the credit to himself. "See, aren't you glad you listened to me? What you needed was to move. It's given you a whole new lease on life."

I could only laugh, and put my arm around his shoulders. "I'm lucky to have a friend like you."

That morning I had awakened with a lick on the cheek from Dude. With the weather cooling off, he was snuggling closer under the covers during the night. I'd grown used to slipping in and out of bed carefully, and rolling over only after checking to see where he was.

He was in a frolicsome mood after my shower, scampering into the bathroom and attacking my underwear, playing I've-got-your-sock-what-are-you-going-to-do-about-it? We sat in the armchair together and enjoyed a little container of yogurt mixed with a spoonful of raspberry jam. Since I didn't have a bookstore shift that day, and the morning clouds were parting to let the sunshine through, I fastened on Dude's little blue harness and locked the apartment door behind us.

We weren't halfway down the hallway when Rudy's door opened. When I told him we were going for groceries, he pulled on his shoes and came with us. We walked down the avenue with Dude strutting ahead of us at the end of his leash, checking all smells, in charge of his humans, his little chest thrust forward in that cocky, saucy way he has, his tireless little legs moving three times as fast as ours.

When we got to the supermarket, I spread my backpack over the grill of the upper basket in my grocery cart, and that's where Dude rode with us, just like he always did, up one aisle and down the other. Something about the hectic shoppers and noise inside there intimidated him, and he was always very quiet while I was shopping. I didn't need much, Rudy added some juice and eggs, I threw in a bag of dog chewies, and completely unsuspecting, we headed toward the line of cashiers at the front of the store.

The man in the spotless white shirt and black tie was waiting for us by the cigarette case at the checkout counter. Rudy was holding Dude in his arms while I handed the clerk my bankcard.

"Excuse me, gentlemen," he said, as we wheeled our cart of groceries over to the side, to pack them into our backpacks. "I'm wondering if you gentlemen saw the notice in our window about service dogs," he said, oily with politeness.

"Well, yes, I did, sir," I began politely. How could we have missed it? It was one of those bold, attention-grabbing signs that appear to shout one thing, while they're really saying another. In large red block letters, it read:

SERVICE DOGS WELCOME

The reason for such an odd announcement only became clear when you read the considerably smaller text just below it, which forbade shoppers to bring in any other kind of dog. The idea of taking two walks every night, one for groceries and one for Dude's daily exercise, was a daunting one, and so I had simply pretended not to notice the sign. "Yes, I did, but…"

Rudy interrupted me. He moved forward and stepped slightly in front of me, as though shielding me. "If you're asking whether my partner and I have AIDS, then the answer is yes."

I was just as shocked as the store manager.

"That's not at all what I…"

"You should be more direct, and say what you mean," said Rudy firmly, without a blink. "And if you're asking if Dude is a service animal, then I'm sure your lawyers will recognize the term, companion animal. He provides what is called emotional support. You may have heard of it. My partner and I would be happy to show you our license for a companion animal. In court."

The man backed away in a stammering rush of apologies.

We squeezed all our groceries into our backpacks, taking turns holding Dude while the other one packed. I waited until we were across the parking lot from the supermarket before I ventured, "I had no idea we were partners."

"Do you mind?"

"Not at all. And since when did you get Dude a license to be a companion animal?"

"Okay, I stretched a few things," he admitted. "But you have to get used to playing the AIDS card. If you've got to have AIDS, you might as well use it."

It was an easy victory. I was starting to feel confident. I had conquered my landlady. I had conquered the supermarket manager. My HIV medication was working wonders. My health was up. My energy was up. And every day now spent with Dude was filled with delight.

But there was one hurdle I had yet to face, and would not be able to get past so easily. The closer I grew to Dude, the more I realized that I could never give him back.

PART THREE

Chapter 22

Call Me Urgent

"They've let him out."

Those were her first words. She didn't even say hello. She knew it was me, and we didn't have time to waste. It sounded like she'd been crying. I tried to pretend at first that I didn't know what she was talking about, but a twisting in my gut told me my worst fears were coming true.

"Taylor?"

"They let him out of jail this morning."

"Talk louder."

"He's pissed as hell about being evicted."

"He's what?"

"He's coming for his dog."

She said something else that I couldn't understand, her words drowned out by the honking of a car horn in the background and the whizzing grumble and roar of Friday morning traffic. It sounded like she was standing on some busy street corner downtown.

She had sent me a text a few minutes before that read:

CALL ME URGENT

I was halfway to work on a bus packed full of sleepy, sullen people, every seat taken, the aisle jammed with standing riders clutching the rails, none of whom wanted to be in that bus. Rain was pecking at the windows, letting us all know that a drenching would be unavoidable the moment we stepped outside.

At first I pretended it wasn't my phone beeping. Then, when it stopped, I discreetly pulled it out of my pocket to see who had texted me. I stared down at her message. I'd been so caught up in my new dog ownership that I hadn't thought about Jade for weeks. I didn't want to call her. I don't like to talk on my cell in public. I'm self-conscious. Besides, I talk too loud. I have a hard time hearing.

I called her anyway, afraid to not know what it was she wanted to tell me. "Talk louder, I can't hear what you're saying."

"He's been texting me all morning." Her voice went up a notch into a less-controllable register. She was breathing in short little gasps, in between wet choking sounds. "He keeps saying how much he loves me, and how he's got to see me. I don't want to see him. I don't want to ever see him again..."

We were disconnected.

Panicking, I called her back. The line was busy.

I stared down at my phone long after losing her. I was stuck, mentally jammed, unable to think clearly. I must have known the day had to come when he would get out of jail. I didn't have permanent ownership. It was only supposed to be for a day or two, before jail-time caused it to be protracted. Was I really about to lose Dude?

What if I didn't play by the rules? What if I decided not to give him back? Would I be in serious danger?

Suddenly the thought of Dude alone in my apartment almost made me physically ill.

I had to get off this bus.

I bumped into the woman beside me, accidentally stepped one someone's foot, and impulsively pulled the bus cord over the window, lighting up the red sign announcing a stop ahead. One passenger on this trainload of the dead would not be going to work this morning.

"Excuse me, excuse me."

The bus pulled over at the next stop to let me off. Extricating myself from the crowded aisle, I landed on the wet morning sidewalk with a jolt, and watched the bus pull away and continue on down the avenue without me.

I had done the unthinkable. I had gotten off the bus to work. For a moment I stood there in the rain stunned by my own audacity. Was it worth risking my job?

All I could think about was getting home fast. I glanced across the street, considered waiting for a bus heading back the way I'd just come from, and then decided I didn't have time to wait at a bus stop and began striding toward home.

The way back took longer than I expected. I arrived home drenched and breathless, fears mounting, and bounded up the back stairs two at a time. I ran down the hall and unlocked my apartment. The moment I swung open the door, Dude came scampering out of the bedroom, his little paws skittering on the wood floor.

"Oh, pooch, I'm so glad you're still here!"

I struggled out of my sopping jacket as I went down on my knees, let him rear up on his hind legs, put his front paws on my chest, and lick me.

I quickly phoned the bookstore and told them I wouldn't be able to come in today. Then I took off my wet clothes and pulled on dry ones. After that I didn't know what to do. I was facing the unimaginable possibility of having this goofy little dog snatched out of my apartment. The very thought of going through life without him made my stomach knot in dread. Dude had showed me how to be happy again, every single day.

But would I fight to keep him?

I wanted to run down the hall to Rudy's, to pound on the door and demand his support, his advice, but he wasn't back from the methadone clinic yet. It was just Dude and me, alone here, against whatever might happen. Taylor could show up any minute and claim his pet. And I would be forced to either fight or give up my little friend.

"Dude, what are we going to do?"

In answer, the little dog took a couple full-length stretches to get the sleepy kinks out of his body, and looked concerned. As well he should be! I'd seen how Taylor treated him. Without a home, living with a temperamental, unpredictable drug dealer on the streets, his doggy life would be a living nightmare. I couldn't let Taylor take him. But how was I going to stop him?

The floor-rattling footfalls of someone running down the hall, then a sudden loud pounding on my door caused me to freeze in terror.

This was it. I was trapped. There was only one way out of here. I would have to face him. Would I fight to keep Dude? Would I?

I tried to bravely fling open the door, to confront him, but my fingers fumbled pathetically with the lock. Then a voice that wasn't Taylor whispered, "It's me. Let me in."

Chapter 23

The Stolen Dog

Jade was barely eighteen, but she didn't look very young at the moment. She looked aged and exhausted and scared, afraid of Taylor and afraid of herself. She was also looking very wet. She pulled the soaked hoodie off her head, but she didn't look much drier underneath. The dripping collar of her overcoat was plastered up around her neck.

Her first greetings were for Dude, who was up on his hind legs in tail-wagging delight. I grabbed two of the biggest towels I could find in the bathroom closet and wrapped them around her, drying her hair and leaving her to do the rest.

"You're drenched."

"I got caught in the worst of it. I've been walking a lot."

"Afraid to go home?"

"I keep seeing him outside my house, across the street waiting for me."

I gave her a T-shirt that was too small for me. She slipped into the bathroom, and came out looking like the little sister I never had. She glanced out the window. "Looks like the rain is over for now. That will make it a little easier."

"Where are you going?"

"Nowhere in particular. Just not home. Just not where he can find me. I'd ask if I could hide out here, except that this is one of the first places he'll come. That's why I can't stay for long. Just long enough to dry out a bit."

We aired out her shoes as best we could and left them in the kitchen, on a chair in front of the open oven. She tucked her bare feet underneath her on the sofa, and I wrapped a blanket around her. When I came back with a glass of orange juice, the blanket bulged and moved strangely. Which explained where Dude was.

We sat together on the sofa, knees to knees, hers wet. "Rudy said he saw you downtown. He told me you're off the stuff."

"I've been clean for three weeks." She tried to keep how proud she was out of her voice. "It's easy now. It was hell for about three days."

"Good for you."

"Which means I don't have to see Taylor anymore. He's lost his big ace. What's he got that I need? I'm through with shooting up," she said aggressively, with a passion and resolve that hinted she might not be as confident as she wanted to sound, "and I'm through with him. Through!"

"You sound like you've got it all figured out," I said. "Don't let anyone talk you out of it."

"Oh, believe me, he tried. You know what Taylor is like. He mumbles all this stuff over the phone, but basically he just wanted to get high and fuck. I really pissed him off when I said no, and he was already super annoyed about being evicted," she said, sniffling. "By the way, he says it's all your fault, that you talked dirt about him to old Mrs Stoll."

"*What?* That's insane!" I couldn't believe she actually said that. "Why would he think that?"

"He said everything was going fine until you moved in, and now you've stolen his dog."

"Stolen? *Stolen?*"

The telephone started ringing.

Jade and I both stared at it. I didn't budge to pick up the receiver. It kept ringing until the phone went to my message machine. Click. No message. Then a moment later it started ringing again. And rang. And rang.

She looked at me. "What are you going to do?"

"I don't really know."

"You need to get out of here."

"How about you?"

"I've got to get back to school before fourth period, or they'll call my Dad."

"What if Taylor shows up at your school?"

She honored me with one of her few smiles. "I'm a clever girl. He'll never catch me."

"Does your Dad know you're in danger?"

"I keep Dad out of my private life. The less he knows, the better. Parents worry too much."

Dude poked his head up out of the blanket, and gave her a lick on the cheek. She snuggled back into the pillows, let her eyes close, and a moment later she was asleep in the warm, dry chair, with a warm, dry dog in her lap...

She awoke with a jolt. "How long have I been here?" she asked in fear. She quickly put on her oven-warmed shoes and damp hoodie, looking skinny and vulnerable and cold. "Go somewhere else, please, don't stay here," were her last words to me.

I should have listened to her.

Chapter 24
Afraid to Go Home

I didn't dare stay at home. I had to get Dude out of there. With the usual struggle and confusion of signals I managed to get him strapped into his little blue harness, hooked on his leash, locked the door of my apartment behind us and headed out into the weather. The rain had eased up for the moment, but the back stairs were slippery and I could see that Dude hated getting his paws wet on the damp sidewalk. He stopped periodically to give his little body a thorough, vigorous shaking.

That day Dude might just as well have been homeless, for all the wandering we did. I gave him a pep talk, tried to sound as confident as I could, and he seemed to understand that the situation was serious. I carried him sometimes and hugged him inside my jacket to keep him warm. We had to keep moving, and be impossible to find. I didn't want to linger anywhere that Taylor could possibly hunt us down. I didn't know where to go and so we just kept changing direction, never staying anywhere long, keeping as much as possible off the grid, cutting through back alleys, crossing streets in unlikely places.

We ended up down in the ravine of Ravenna Park, strolling for several hours through the restful shade of the dripping trees. I'd stuffed my pockets full of doggie treats, so I made sure Dude didn't get hungry. He drank from the shallow creek beside the main trail along the ravine bottom.

Beyond the park, we strolled past schoolyards and down tree-lined neighborhood streets, keeping off the main highways where buses passed, avoiding anywhere Taylor might be looking for us.

By afternoon we started getting hungry. I stopped in a pizza shop on the Ave and bought a slice to eat sitting on a stool outside, dropping Dude the biggest pieces of sausage. We took our time. I let him sniff and explore wherever he wanted to go. I was afraid to go back to the house. I didn't want Dude to be anywhere he could be snatched.

Around six in the evening, sitting on a bench in a small park and starting to feel a chill in the air, I phoned Jade to find out if she'd seen him.

"He's pissed because he can't find you," she whispered into her phone. "I wouldn't tell him anything. He's acting like we were all stabbing him in the back while he was in jail."

"Where is he now, do you know?"

"He's out looking for you." She pressed the phone to her chest and he could hear her muffled voice yelling, "It's for me, Dad. No, I haven't. Just a second." Then she whispered, "I can't talk now. I'm grounded. My father's being a jerk. Be careful," and disconnected.

Dude and I wandered through the park until the ravine became too dark and we no longer felt safe there. Then we headed up to the avenue and made our way past the taverns and used clothing shops, pizza places and banks and Thai cafes that crowded along the sidewalk beneath the streetlamps. We looked in store windows and read sandwich boards. As long as no other dogs were in sight, Dude behaved like a calm, sensible, rational being. I could stop to let old ladies and children pet him. But sooner or later we would be exhausted with only one place left to go. As hard as it was to lower my vigilance, to dare to relax, I started trying to convince myself that the worst was over.

We stopped across the street from the Stolls' house, hesitating on the corner just out of range of the streetlamp. Peering up through the maple branches, no lights could be seen from the front. Keeping to the other side of the street, we walked around to the alley and looked up at the house from behind.

The second floor windows and the window in the upstairs door were brightly lit, like beacons into the night.

Had I forgotten to turn off the hall light when I left? I scowled in concentration, trying to remember. The hall light? the hall light? I almost always turned it off. I was fairly certain I had flipped the switch as Dude and I headed out the door and down the stairs.

But maybe not.

Maybe I meant to, and got distracted. Then again, maybe someone had gone up there to find me and turned it on. Maybe someone was still up there waiting for me.

A neighbor out walking her dog rounded the corner of the block. The sight of her triggered the usual seismic upheaval in Dude's behavior, a sudden volley of psychotic barking, tugging and straining on his leash as though he'd become possessed.

It was one of those moments in which that little dog became incomprehensible. I couldn't even guess his motives for feeling the need to make such an outspoken, inexplicable racket. I managed to quiet him down, but not before he had awakened every dog on the street, and several frenzied cousins locked inside various houses along the tree-lined way could be heard becoming equally upset and joining their supportive voices to the free-for-all.

"Well, if Taylor is up there waiting for us," I thought grimly, "he certainly knows we're coming."

I opened the gate into the yard, trying to keep it from squeaking, and started up the stairs. I was tired of walking. I was tired of being afraid.

Too worn out to be careful any longer, I trudged up the staircase, trying to keep up with Dude on his leash, convinced that I had suffered enough, that if Taylor wasn't there by now he wasn't coming tonight, and that I had more than earned a restful night's sleep.

Chapter 25

What Happened to Rudy

No sooner did I unlock the outside door to the second floor hallway and unfasten Dude's leash than he bolted down the hall straight into Rudy's apartment.

Rudy's door was open. Sometimes he did that to entice me into visiting him, but this time I heard groaning coming from inside, and that was all it took to make me break into a panicky run.

The first thing I saw going in was the broken floor lamp. The coffee table was turned on its side, with something dark sopping into the carpet beneath it. A shelf of paperbacks had been knocked to the floor, along with a pile of comics out of the windowsill in slippery plastic sleeves.

I found him curled up on the floor in a corner of his bedroom, on the other side of the rumpled bed, making horrible moaning sounds, his bathrobe ripped down the front, his shoulder scratched, with Dude already ministering his attentions, frantically whimpering and sniffing and licking him. Rudy had a purple bruise on his cheek that looked like it would turn into a fine black eye, and a mouthful of blood that kept dribbling over his lips whenever he opened his mouth to try to talk.

"Ouch ouch ouch!"

I scooted Dude to one side and knelt beside him. "Do you need a doctor?"

He made sounds deep in his mouth. A thread of blood ran down from the corner of his lip. His mumbled answer was emphatically negative. I made out the words, "No insurance."

I rose to my feet, anxious to do something. I couldn't tell if there were any broken bones or internal damage. "Is there someone I should call?"

"Forget it. ... fine."

He mumbled something else I couldn't hear. He rubbed his jaw, and winced. "That asshole really bashed me."

Weakly, still obviously in a lot of pain, he tried to scramble up onto his knees. I caught him before he could fall, then supported him as he used my shoulder to work his way up onto his feet. We shuffled into the bathroom, with Dude scurrying around our legs, where Rudy washed his face gently over the sink, leaving wet pink and red splotches over everything. He looked at his battered face in the mirror, and whimpered.

"Was it Taylor?"

He touched his cheeks gingerly, to make sure the teeth were still firmly placed. "You just missed him."

"But why would he do this to you?"

In answer, he made a sound that might have been a laugh. Then, with great difficulty over each word, he said, "He wants to know where his dog is."

We both looked down at Dude, who looked back at us quizzically, his tail suddenly wagging, eager to play and hoping treats were involved.

I tried to harden myself against the chill those words caused in me. "What did you tell him?"

"Nothing. That's what pissed him off."

"I can't believe he did this to you."

"He'll do the same to you." He flexed his arms and legs, making sure nothing was broken. "Listen, we've got to get out of here. Rent a hotel room for a couple days."

"You've got to be joking. I'm just a bookseller, man. I don't have that kind of money."

"I know where we can stay. Do you have a gun?"

"A real one? Are you kidding? I've never even *seen* a real gun. I'm not going to shoot anybody. We're going to call the police like two sane human beings…"

"Oh, no, we're not. No police."

I wanted to laugh, but it wasn't really funny. "Come on, Rudy, talk sense. You've just been beaten up. We're obviously in danger..."

"Listen, there are a few things you don't know about me. I've got nine hundred dollars in traffic tickets I've never paid. The police will not be contacted."

He picked up the phone off the floor, and punched in a number. At first, I thought he had changed his mind and was actually calling the police. Instead he said, "Hey, sweetie, yeah I know, I know, nice to hear your voice, too. Listen, me and my buddy need a place to crash tonight. You mind if we stay at your place?" He listened briefly, then said, "Great. We're on our way. Oh, and there's a dog." An objection was raised. "A very, very *little* dog. Okay, see ya in a few."

He disconnected, and turned to me. "Let's get out of here. That jerk could come back any minute. One visit from him tonight was enough." He began punching another number into my phone. "I'm calling a taxi. It's not that far, but I'm in no condition to walk. Grab whatever you're going to need for a couple days, and make it fast. We've got to get down those back stairs, and I'm going to need a little help."

With every passing minute, I dreaded Taylor's arrival. Slowly I managed to get both Dude and Rudy down the back stairs and waiting in front of the house when the taxi pulled up. Punctuated by Rudy's groans, the elderly Nigerian driver and I managed to get him into the back seat, all the while insisting that he didn't need a doctor. I was just getting ready to slide in beside him and close the back door of the cab when the leash was jerked out of my hand.

"Dude, come back here!"

He had seen another dog across the street. Barking insanely, he was now charging toward him. Screaming Dude's name, I lunged down the sidewalk after him. He had gone deaf, for all the effect my cries were having on him. With no regard for either of the two cars coming toward us, Dude bolted into the street, skittering between them, dragging the leash behind him. My wails had no effect.

In a moment, Dude was out of sight.

I ran back to the waiting taxi. "Listen, go to your friend's. I'll call you as soon as I find Dude, and we'll join you there."

Rudy wanted to stay, but the driver already had the meter running. "Don't worry," I said, far more confident than I was, "he'll come to his senses. He'll hear me calling him. I'll phone you when I've got him."

The taxi set off down the street into the shadow of the maple trees. I began striding in the other direction, calling Dude, my stomach in a knot of anxiety, my fears piling on top of each other with nowhere to go.

"Dude, come back here!" I called into the night.

No answer.

Chapter 26

The Drug Dealer's Dog

I walked the streets of the neighborhood for over an hour, calling his name. No response. Finally I gave up and went home and waited. He had no collar. People stole Chihuahuas all the time. I was a wreck. Regardless of any threat from Taylor, I propped open the hall door, left my own door open, and though I turned off all the lights, I sat waiting in my armchair, hoping against hope. I let myself break down in tears in the dark. How could I have let the leash get pulled out of my hand?

I was too miserable to sleep, but I must have dozed off briefly, because the next thing I knew Dude was running down the hall toward me, dragging his leash behind him.

It took about a minute of sobbing relief before I came to my senses, closed the hall door, and then my own. His return was just short of miraculous. He looked a little muddy and wet and smelled of unpleasant decomposing things, but I was so glad to have him back I didn't care. I was just about to phone Rudy to tell him the good news, that Dude was fine and we were on our way, when I heard the door at the far end of the hall open and close.

The footsteps that should have followed didn't happen. The hall was unnaturally silent.

Slowly rising to my feet, I stopped breathing and listened intently.

Now I could hear the groan of the floorboards, the creaking that always happened in these old houses under footsteps. His footsteps. Who else would be walking down our hall at this hour? Creak, creak. I waited for the knock, dreading it.

The knocking didn't come.

Something shifted outside in the hallway. I stood motionless, in the middle of the living room. I could see the hall light shining under the door, and then something moved through the light.

Someone was standing just outside my door.

A floorboard creaked.

I tried frantically to remember: Did I lock it? Did I lock it? I usually did automatically, but sometimes I forgot. Why didn't I think of that before? What a dolt I was! Locking the door was one of those repetitious, mechanical activities that one's body learned to do without contact with the brain. Sometimes I felt so safe I just forgot to be careful. I'd never had any real reasons to be afraid, before tonight.

Someone knocked. The door rattled with the impact. Someone on the other side wanted me to know that I was summoned. I jerked back, away from the doorway, genuinely terrified.

"I know you're in there," said a voice I recognized with a chill. "I know you're waiting for me. Well, here I am. The wait is over. Aren't you glad to see me?"

I've never been that afraid in my life. My lips opened and shut, as though I were saying something, but nothing came out.

"Don't I deserve a little friendlier welcome home than this? I thought we were friends."

The voice paused, as though waiting for me to contribute something. I might have spoken, if I could have moved my jaw.

Suddenly the doorknob twisted and turned.

Locked.

He made a soft, animal sound of frustration. "You do realize there's no way you can get out without going past me."

By then I'd been quiet for too long. Now I didn't know how to explain myself or where to start. I was so scared I was getting a massive headache.

"I'm very patient," he said at last, breaking the silence. "I can wait you out. I'm not in any rush. I've got all the time in the world. You wanna learn about time, you should try being in jail. I've been in jail for ninety days. That's one hell of a long time. Now that I'm free, I want to be happy. I want to play with my dog."

I frantically tried to think of something to say.

"Hey, Dude," he called softly, in his most charming voice. "Are you in there? *Dude!*"

Dude barked.

I could hear him softly chuckling. "That's my boy. Now, open up this door."

I tried to say something. My mouth opened, my lips moved, but nothing came out.

"This is a very old house," said Taylor. "You know, I'll bet these locks aren't very strong. And these old doorframes – you know how old this wood must be? I wouldn't want to damage Mrs Stoll's door."

I took a step backward. "Don't, Taylor." The words came out so softly I wasn't sure he heard me.

"If you force me to, I will."

For a long moment there was a strained, dreadful stillness.

Then an ear-splitting, battering crash.

The door banged inward, clattering against the door stop, the lock half torn out amid splintering wood.

Taylor Gates slowly lowered his foot to the floor. He smiled at me, sweaty and scruffy and unshaved, but he wasn't really looking at me. He was looking down at the little dog cowering behind me. His face looked genuinely flushed with happiness. "Hey, Dude buddy, how's it goin'? Did you miss Daddy? Do you want to go for a ride?"

Dude's tail started wagging.

"Leave him alone, Taylor."

He gave me that terrible smile, with dark eyes that seemed to be laughing. "He's happy to see me. You seem to be forgetting that he's my dog. I can do whatever I want with him."

"You abandoned him. You never came back for him. He's not your dog anymore."

He was no longer smiling. "I was in jail, you asshole. Now get out of my way. Dude is going with me."

"He has a good home here."

"His home is wherever I am, you fag."

I was so busy keeping myself out of his reach that I didn't realize what he was doing until he lunged forward and snatched up Dude in one quick swoop. The little dog gave a yelp of terror, squealing and kicking in his arms.

"Put him down, you fucker!" I shouted and grabbed both his arms to pry them off the flailing, struggling dog. He was so much stronger than me it was a joke. One arm came away from gripping Dude and dealt me such a backhanded blow across the face that my head went backward faster than my feet could move.

I sat down hard, hitting the back of my head on the wooden arm of the sofa. For a second, I didn't know where I was. Then I heard Dude yelp, that's all it took to get me struggling dizzily to my feet.

I was so busy shouting, "Leave him alone!" that I didn't think about dodging his kick until the heel of his foot collided with my ribs.

I hit the floor harder the second time, whacking the back of my head against the wall as I went down. By this time my poor battered head was throbbing. His kick was so unexpected that I curled up like a slug in salt, unable to breathe. He followed it with another kick that was worse. I was hurting in so many places I couldn't figure out how to get back up on my feet, while Dude squirmed and barked for all he was worth, with a heart-splitting squeal of terror.

"Put down that dog," said a booming voice behind us. "Kick him one more time, and I'll shoot off your foot."

Elderly Mrs Stoll stood in the doorway, wearing what looked like a violet flannel nightdress patterned with little pink roses, holding what looked very much like a real, functioning gun pointed directly at us, gripped at the end of her two trembling, skinny, brittle arms.

"I said, put down that dog."

I'd led a sheltered life. I'd never seen an actual revolver that worked, and there was one right in front of me, up close and personal. How ironic that it would enter my life in the hands of an old woman! Though her bony arms trembled, her finger on the trigger looked like she meant business and knew what to do.

Taylor slowly set down Dude, never taking his eyes off Mrs Stoll. The little dog leaped into my arms, trembling.

"You no longer live here," Mrs Stoll said firmly, her eyes scowling in concentration as she watched every move he made. "You have been evicted. Your things are down in the basement storage. You have no business here."

"I came for my dog," he said, taking an aggressive step toward her. "He's my property. You can't stop me from taking what's mine."

"Your dog?" Mrs Stoll was momentarily confounded, and looked to me for some kind of explanation. So did Taylor, with a sneer of triumph. Dude whimpered and squirmed and began earnestly licking my neck and ear. Unfortunately, the one thing I knew for certain was that Dude did *not* belong to me. I was powerless. But maybe I could keep him out of Taylor's hands.

I struggled painfully to my feet.

"Legally, the dog belongs to Rudy," I said, with slow and measured words. That caught both Taylor and Mrs Stoll off-guard. "Rudy is the one who signed the papers."

"Fuck you," said Taylor. "You know that doesn't mean a thing."

"Legally it does. You couldn't sign for Dude because you didn't have ID."

"Fuck you," said Taylor.

"So he is not your dog," said Mrs Stoll. "Look at him! Poor dog, you frighten him. Leave, before I shoot you."

"I don't think you'll shoot me," he sneered.

"Leave, or you will find out," said Mrs Stoll.

For one terrible moment the three of us stood suspended, each of us watching the other two to see who would first break the tableau. A drop of sweat trickled down the side of Taylor's cheek and hung shivering on his handsome jaw. Slowly the wrinkle lines converging on his eyes tightened into a humorless smile.

"I'm not leaving without what's mine," said Taylor. "I don't have much, but I damn well have that dog. Dude loves me, and he's going with me. I don't think you'll be shooting anyone, you silly old goat." He strode suddenly toward her, his arm out to snatch the gun away from her.

Mrs Stoll pulled the trigger.

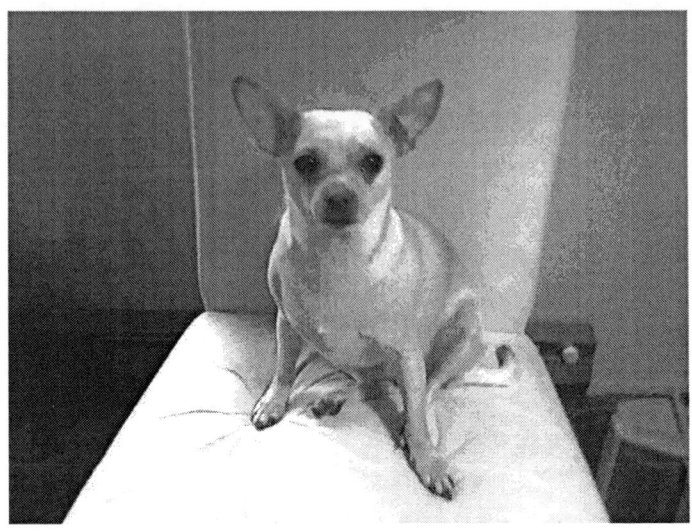

Chapter 27
Render Unto Caesar

The day was ugly to begin with, thick with dark clouds and getting darker, with hot, dirty rain congesting the sky. All morning I had been miserable, and finally just confronted myself and admitted what I knew was true. I had to live with myself, and no matter how I justified what I was doing, I knew it was wrong.

I had taken his dog. It was my fault he'd been shot. He might be a monster, he might deserve to be shot, but I was nobody's judge and stealing was stealing, no matter who you stole from. I was a kinder and smarter owner, I could give Dude a better life, but he simply wasn't mine. Soon I wouldn't even be able to look at Dude without feeling like I'd kidnapped the most precious thing that a scumbag like Taylor Gates would ever possess. What happened last night just showed how very wrong I could be.

I tugged my way into my fleece, and pulled a stocking cap down over my ears. The weather was going to get nasty, but that wasn't going to stop me. I had to face the truth, before my guilt ate me alive. I would offer to buy him. It was the only honest thing I could do. I had to gamble that the answer wouldn't be no.

Dude scampered around to block me from going, or at least to remind me to take him along. He looked up at me with what we called his laughing face, mouth open and panting, eager and ready to head out on an adventure, even if it was only a walk through the neighborhood.

"Sorry, buddy, I can't this time." I was barely able to get the words out. "They don't allow dogs in the hospital – not even dogs as cute as you." I scratched him behind those big, funny ears of his and then slid quickly out the door.

I didn't tell anyone I was going. Friends always think you need to be tough, stand your ground, show self-respect, don't compromise, grab what you deserve. But I couldn't escape the knowledge that in Taylor's mind the dog had always belonged to him. I couldn't escape the possibility that maybe, in his own way, Taylor loved that dog, too.

You would think a gunshot might have solved it all.

Instead watching someone get shot, watching Taylor yelping like a dog while he thrashed about on the floor clutching his thigh, bleeding and in pain there in my apartment, watching him twitching and crying, had raised the question of just how far I would go to keep something that wasn't mine. Mr Stoll had already called 9-1-1. The medics came. The police came. He was taken away. The questioning lasted into the night. Dude retreated into the bedroom and burrowed deep under the covers, which was where I found him when I finally got to bed.

The poor little dog had yelped when the gun was fired, and at first I'd been terrified that he had been hit. I had to watch him shake with fear afterward. Hugging him to drive away the trembling, I could no longer ignore the depths of my own wrong-headedness, my determination to have what wasn't mine at any cost.

The truth might be painful and unfair, but it was simple and clear and unavoidable. Taylor had asked me to take care of Dude, and I had decided to keep him. No matter how Dude and I might feel about the situation, he was not mine. Either I had to make him mine, or I had to give him up.

I had checked my bank account. I knew exactly how much I had. If necessary, my parents would loan me money. I would pay whatever Taylor asked. My only fear was that he would refuse to sell him.

Even though I was hungry, I had been too upset to eat breakfast. I dressed mechanically. Then I wasted almost an hour standing in front of the mirror, but I could no longer see myself. All I could do was replay last night over and over, and one thing was for sure: if I had given Taylor back what belonged to him, if I had done something sensible like offering to buy the dog, Taylor would not have been shot. I had to make the situation good somehow, no matter how much it cost, no matter how righteous I felt.

I stared straight ahead in the bus. I didn't look into anyone's eyes getting on or getting off.

The #49 only takes you so far, and then you have to get out and walk about half a mile, down Broadway and then around and down the curves of Seneca to get to Virginia Mason Hospital. I must have walked it, because I got there. Some guy was sitting at the piano in the lobby, playing something sad. I ignored him. I knew where I was going, and I felt like I had to get there.

My stomach rumbled and tossed as I walked down the hall teeming with people in white jackets, keeping my eyes away from the nurses and orderlies, not to mention the dozens of visitors hiding their secret griefs, people with lumps in their throats, all trying not to show their fear. I walked past them, dodging hospital equipment on wheels full of hoses and dials and inflatable bags, focusing on the numbers posted outside each door.

I needn't have bothered. The policeman standing outside one of the doors gave it away.

He recognized me from the Stolls' house. We exchanged a few words, but I don't remember what they were. I was too busy staring past him through the open doorway at the bandaged figure lying in the bed at the far end of the room.

I waited for his head to turn in my direction. I wasn't sure he'd want my company.

No one else was there. The other bed was empty. He didn't see me approaching where he lay stretched out by the window, confined by the bed's metal bars. I stood at the foot of his bed. His eyes slowly turned to focus on me. His bandaged leg was raised and suspended. His hands remained under the blankets. I wondered if he was handcuffed. For a long time neither one of us could say a word. When I finally managed to speak, what came out wasn't so bright.

"I never thought she'd pull the trigger," I said stupidly.

He smiled crookedly with pain. "Neither did I."

That was pretty much the extent of our conversation. After that, there was only the final matter to be settled. I stood there trying to find the words to say, until I finally blurted out, "Please, I want to buy your dog."

He rolled his head to look at me.

"You can have everything I've got in my bank account. Really. It would be worth it to me. Would three hundred dollars be enough?"

At first I thought he wasn't going to answer. "I don't want your money."

It was what I had feared. I felt my body turning cold. I quickly added, "I know three hundred isn't enough. But I could make payments. However much you want. I don't care, I'll pay it. Six hundred for a Chihuahua? Isn't that about right? Or how about seven?"

I couldn't read his eyes. They were dead cold. I couldn't tell if he even saw me standing there, if he could hear what I was saying.

"Just don't take him away from me." My voice was starting to crack now. "Please. When you get out of the hospital, when you get out of jail, don't come to get your dog back. Because, because I could never... because I love him too much and... I can't give him back..."

I couldn't go on. The words wouldn't come out. They were the truth, but I choked on them deep in my throat.

Taylor spoke instead, slowly and with difficulty. "I may be an asshole, but I'm not stupid. Keep him. Now, get the fuck out of here. I don't want to ever see you again."

The black, swollen rainclouds choking the sky finally broke, drenching the city. By the time I found standing room on the bus, trembling with sheer emotional exhaustion, I was soaked to the skin. I hardly noticed.

I ran all the way home from the bus stop.

Fumbling with my key in the lock, I could hear him on the other side of the door scratching and thudding against the wood. I took two steps into my apartment and dropped down onto my knees, dripping wet, and let him jump into my arms and lick me all over the face. I didn't mind when he stuck his tongue up my nostrils, and between my lips, and licked the tears running down my cheeks.

Dude was mine.

*

Rough Draft 26 February, 4-6 July2011
First Version 6, 16-24 Sept 11
Second Version 28 Sept – 5 Oct 11
Third Version 8 Oct 11
Fourth Version 11-26 Oct 11
Fifth Version 5-12 November 11

Revised Sixth Version 19-26 November 11